The Reputation

The Reputation

Bjarni Bjarnason

translated by
David McDuff

First published as *Mannorð* in 2011 by Uppheimar
This translation published by **Red Hand Books**
part of Red Hand Media Ltd
Flexadux House, Grange Road
Gainsborough DN21 1QB

www.redhandbooks.co.uk

Mannorð © Bjarni Bjarnason
Translated by David McDuff
This translation copyright *The Reputation* © 2017 Red Hand Books
All rights in the works printed here revert to the authors,
translators and original copyright holders after publication

This edition: ISBN 978-1-910346-19-8

Prepared for publication by Red Hand Books
Cover design by Rachel Bennett © red hand media ltd

Cattle die, kindred die
Every man is mortal
But the good name never dies
Of one who has done well

Hávamál

1

Sitting at the hotel bar Starkaður Levi looked pensively into his glass. That morning he had received a message from Janus Andersen, his lawyer in London, to the effect that the Icelandic state prosecutor was demanding his immediate return for questioning about the collapse of the banks. Sipping brandy in time to his hard-drinking reflection, he noticed some Icelanders at the corner table, an elderly married couple and their middle-aged female friend in a nautical cap. As he had for more than a year now, he introduced himself as Charles P. Harvey, from Guernsey in the Channel Islands. Said he had done business with Icelanders over the years and found it a positive experience.

Soon he had impressed them with a thorough knowledge of Iceland, and they told him the story of their travels. They had been on a round-the-world cruise which had begun in a carefree spirit, but because of the situation at home which froze their bank accounts, were now scavenging for food and unable to put into port under their real name here in Kochi; the yacht would have been detained and confiscated. Starkaður gave them advice on how they could obtain documents to overcome the problem, and they were so bowled over that he became complacent in the role. When amid a story he mimicked the former Icelandic prime minister's memorable television address in which he asked God to bless Iceland, and then forgot to switch straight back into English, there was silence at the table. Then the trio backed away, and the lady in the cap snapped at him that she could not believe it, she had been sipping beer with the worst traitor in Icelandic history, spat in his face and poured the contents of her glass over his shoes. While he wiped his face, she showered him with abuse, culminating in a statement that she wanted nothing more to do with a scoundrel who had helped to bring about the breakup of both her family and her homeland. Demanded that he give her his wallet, because she owned more of what was in it than he did. When she attempted to feel inside his jacket he seized her hand. Before he knew it a glass of red wine had smashed on top of his head. Upstairs in the hotel suite he pulled fragments of glass from his scalp as he cursed deeply in Icelandic for the first time in a long while. His hair was matted with blood and wine.

After taking a bath, putting on his pyjamas and lying down under the covers to feel sorry for himself, he suddenly had an unexpected fit of the giggles. The cursing's of the woman in the cap ran through his mind, making him shake with laughter until he abruptly fell silent. He envisioned something harsh and cold, and missed the hauteur of the Icelandic landscape. Suddenly he felt there was something very appealing about the lady in the cap, and felt it crucially important to tell her that it was why he had sat down at their table. Rather than argue among themselves, they should look to the fact that they were fellow countrymen in distress on foreign soil. He could even throw in his lot with them and be at their service, as he was a seasoned mariner. He put on some formal clothes, had a brandy, went down to the hotel bar and looked for the enemy. A clean cloth had appeared on the corner table, and the trio were gone. As he went up in the lift, the sense of loneliness that had receded during the altercation flooded over him again. Back in his suite he muttered to empty leather armchairs that it was worse to be ignored by folk to whom it was a matter of complete indifference whether he drew breath or not than to be hated by his own people. He dug out his old passport, fired up his computer and booked a flight home. In the hope of regaining the love and respect of his compatriots by showing public remorse, he wrote an article under the heading *We Did Our Best*, which appeared in the country's most widely read newspaper on the day he landed at Keflavík airport. In it he said that when the system collapsed the crisis had been unmanageable, admitted the mistakes of all the Icelandic bankers, and asked for forgiveness.

On the weekend before his detention and questioning, he put a six-pack of beer in a briefcase and looked forward to meeting old colleagues at a housewarming party. He had not been in the country since the financial collapse, and he found the atmosphere unrecognizable. People said that the article, which had been the subject of much discussion in the media, showed he still thought he was such a big shot that he was on a par with the nation to which he talked down like an ex-girlfriend in a bitter breakup. Soon the guests became tipsy and took turns to mock the 'confession', as someone called the article. A fellow with green tinted sunglasses on the tip of his nose and a Hammer of Thor on a chain around his neck got up on a chair and said that everyone knew Icelandic businessmen could be divided into two groups: those whom Starkaður Levi had already stabbed in the back, and those whom he was going to stab in the back. To this they drank a toast.

Starkaður contemplated the weary speaker and his forcedly cheerful smile, dimly recalled having seen him before. After inquiring about his name, he remembered having done business with him six years earlier. Back then the man had worn a vastly expensive wedding ring, which had now disappeared along with most of his hair. The next weather-beaten orator could not suppress a giggle when he explained that several members of the financial sector held an annual golf tournament at Nesvöllur called 'StarkStick'. The prize was a beautiful hand-made dagger with a blood-red point. He addressed his giggling words specifically to Starkaður, and asked if they could invite him to come and present the award after their next meeting in August. After all, the competition was named after him. To applause, Starkaður bowed and said it was a great honour. He had always tried to encourage walking between holes, it made for a good life for men, anyway. Of course, he attended, and presented the prize to those who were best at this remarkable sport that was so reminiscent of the fact that life is a civilized conflict between dear companions. When last year's winner went home to fetch the prize dagger in order to show it to interested guests, Starkaður sneaked away from the festivities unnoticed.

Three weeks later, after having had a finger broken by an old schoolmate who said he would give him a thorough introduction to a golden shower if he saw him again in the country, having made a mess of things for his ex-girlfriend by trying to support her financially, been beaten up while out on the town and harassed by strangers several times a day, he never left the house unless in disguise.

He had the typical appearance of an Icelandic male, tall, slim with fair hair, but still found it hard to blend so well into the crowd that he could go unnoticed. Assuming a serious disguise was too much trouble, and sometimes merely led to situations where he looked ridiculous. Experience showed that it was better to dress down, look unfashionable and slack-postured; be hunched and dorkish. His jacket sleeves and trouser legs were a few centimetres too short and there were little paint marks on the most threadbare shirt he had found in the Red Cross Shop on Garðastræti Street. There he also bought shoes so worn at the heels that he looked as though he had badly splayed feet. His mobile phone was outmoded and had no Internet, his watch a scratched piece of junk he had dug up at Kolaportið flea market. Along with a rusty twelve year old Volvo sedan that had dirty dice dangling from the rear-view mirror, and a German accent when things got tight, this garb carried him through the days without anyone giving him a second glance. On the rare occasions when he was noticed, people were uncertain about who he was, which ensured him the necessary leeway to make himself disappear.

Although Starkaður wanted to move undisturbed around Reykjavík, the city of his youth, this was no sort of life. He had always talked to a lot of people during a day, and did not enjoy being silent from morning to night among folk he generally felt were chattering a great deal of nonsense. Sometimes, when he sat in a café and eavesdropped on conversations while pretending to be reading the newspaper or surfing the Web, he imagined what he would contribute to the discussion if he were part of the gang and still thought important. Although this was less bad than pretending to be Charles P. Harvey, wandering aimlessly around the globe and lying about the past to new drinking buddies each weekend, he missed chatting normally with his countrymen.

After his reputation had been confiscated, he took a different view of mankind. Reputation seemed to be for the soul as health was for the body, such an obvious blessing that people did not appreciate it until they had lost it. He gazed at people as if bent on spotting the integrity in their behaviour, and caught himself longing to be like normal men. To be one of the many to whom people listened instinctively and respected without even paying heed to. To whom women opened their hearts and with whom they cuddled. In whose lap children settled automatically and became more themselves when they talked to them, whose attention they even fought for. When he sat with his grey character glasses at Café Súfistinn in the Iða bookstore, so bearded that his mouth was scarcely visible, he keenly watched casual and bohemian men who were beautifully unshaven, tastefully lacking in style, and beloved by all. He eavesdropped as they debated contemporary issues and told anecdotes about people. Even the waitresses served them with a secret glint in their eyes, as though they belonged to another, more compassionate world.

Still, most probably they were hardly aware that they led meaningful lives and were sitting on golden reputations. The words of a famous economist to the effect that the value of a stainless reputation could be set at two hundred thousand dollars came back to him. Compared to the sums he had lost in the last two years two hundred thousand dollars was small change. However, of the things he had lost, his reputation was the one thing that he missed.

*

After some time at Súfistinn, Starkaður noticed an author who sat stoop-shouldered with a pair of small reading glasses on his nose and who strangely pursed his lips when concentrating. About him there was such calm that he seemed to vanish into the heart of the atmosphere, both closing a door and locking it behind him. Starkaður stared at him in particular because he had a clear memory of the man's photo on the front page of a newspaper. He had been arrested by policewomen for taking part in protest clashes outside the Parliament. Under the photo it said that he had helped to set fire to the Austurvöllur Centre square Christmas tree, the annual gift from the city of Oslo.

12

The author sat on a long green sofa where there were five circular tables in a row, and never seemed to notice who was sitting beside him. He was often alone for an hour or so, but several times during the day all kinds of people appeared and sat down beside him. When they greeted him, a smile emerged slowly from a great depth, and his eyes required time to get used to a new environment. Coming and going, people engaged him in discussion, told stories, laughed and hugged him. Most often members of the Dream Club came to see him. They recounted their dreams, which he interpreted for them. Then they told stories that were often about the events surrounding the protests and the author's heroic incarceration. He wore a green checked shirt with a black cravat, leaning forward over the table while the club members listened attentively. Once Starkaður managed to tune into the frequency range, the author's voice was low but clear. On this occasion the author said that their mutual friend, Klemmsi, had brought his pals along to his place for an after-party. These were lads alongside whom he had fought the cops in the Parliament gardens and got to know without ever talking to them until that night. One was a little guy who turned out to have wandered around Asia for six months, now writing a travel book and making his living as a journalist. The other was a cannabis-smoking conspiracy theorist whose father was a famous punk rocker, and already famous on that account alone. Early on during the party it was clear that these were to be the future leaders of the nation after the revolution they had evidently been planning. They had begun to collect surplus timber to build barricades, and had filled cans of gasoline for making Molotov cocktails. The author said he was honoured to raise a glass with the founding fathers of the future state, and asked them how they were going to implement the coup.

'They were going to start by staging a shoot-out in the suburb of Mosfellssveit so that the counter-terrorism unit would be called in. Then, when most of the police had gone a long way out into the countryside they were going to close off Vesturlandsvegur Road so that the police could not get back again quickly. To ensure that the traffic would be completely disrupted they were going to order pizzas from all the pizza joints in town. The idea was that there would be so many pizza deliveries on the roads that the police would be unable to make any progress. Then they were going to send dozens of people into the liquor and grocery stores to loot as much alcohol, soft drinks and candy as possible. Meanwhile, people with foreign loans which had multiplied until they were unmanageable would go crowding into the banks and demand all the cash. They were convinced that if there were enough of them, the looting of shops and banks would go peacefully, and the salespeople, cashiers and security guards would not show resistance since they were in the same boat as the revolutionaries.

'At around teatime everyone was to meet on Austurvöllur square. By then the pizzas would have finally got through the traffic blocks. Everyone would get a slice with as much alcohol as they wanted. Banknotes would be showered on the masses from the windows of Hotel Borg. A large TV screen hung in front of Parliament for they were going to occupy the television news studio and give a revolutionary speech that would be broadcast live. Their descriptions slowed down at this point, as they began to argue about which of them should give the speech.'

The author passed a hand through his curly fair hair. Was reflective, though the club members were amused when he mimicked the conspiracy theorists arguing about which of them would be the better revolutionary orator.

'When the revels on Austurvöllur reached their climax, they were going to storm into the Parliament building and set up a disco in the debating chamber to celebrate the end of the capitalist economic system in the country.

'I felt like telling the young pups what I thought of the plan. But I let it be. All I could think of began with the words: 'Well, lads, listen carefully now.' I couldn't help yawning non-stop. To get rid of them I said that unfortunately I had a deadline to meet for an article about child-rearing, stood up and began to make myself scarce. In the hallway, I wished them good luck in their struggle, and then took my leave of them their way with a clenched fist salute. Then I threw myself on the bed, mightily relieved to be free of the founding fathers of the country's future.'

The members of the Dream Club discussed how estranged from reality young radicals were today and what would actually need to be done in order to take over society, were that to be the goal. No matter which of them spoke, it was to the author that most gazes went. Deep down the members seemed to agree that the final authority lay with him. The author seemed to understand neither this trust nor how good his life was. Still less did he realize that he was sitting on a two hundred-thousand-dollar reputation which, with the right pricing, it would be a simple matter to multiply in value until the cash came flowing in.

Starkaður watched the laughing club members insult each other with humorous anecdotes. He sighed, and contemplated the shadow of his coffee cup, reflecting that he no longer wore the stultifying green prison uniform, no longer watched the darkness moving up the walls of the isolation cell. But he might just as well have done. From the moment, he was brought in for questioning by the prosecutor and sentenced to four days' detention, he calculated that it would take the justice system two years to completely destroy his reputation and then sequestrate his house in Thingholt, his bungalow in Hellnar, his cars and other traceable property in Iceland. Until then, he would be a secret visitor not only here in Súfistinn but even in his own home, until he merged with the anonymous night.

His life was over in this country, and there, right in front of his nose, lay the perfect life of an author, an untouchable emblem of meaningful freedom. There was a voice that was listened to, a precious channel for a creative vision of recent historical events.

Their dreams now interpreted, the members of the Dream Club stood up one after the other, ready for the day. When the author was left alone at the table, he picked up his diary and wrote in it for a while. Between paragraphs he smiled, and Starkaður guessed that he was making a note of something related to his recent meeting with the club members. After writing a full stop with a determined gesture and closing the pen with a click, he fished out a pack of Camels, sniffed it thoughtfully, stood up and walked towards the escalator that led down into the bookshop.

On the sofa next to Starkaður the diary lay open. The author had not closed it, presumably to let the ink dry. Starkaður was fascinated by the text, from which wafted a fresh breath from another world. As if through it a tunnel opened on a world of possibilities. He longed to know how someone who had a rich and meaningful life wrote about it for himself. What was this famous protester's opinion of people like him? Was the author one of those folks who yearned to break a wine-glass on his head or plunge a dagger in his back?

A pile of older diaries lay on an empty chair. After hesitating for quite a while, and keeping an eye on the guests around him, Starkaður reached for one of them and sneaked it under his belt beneath his jacket. The feeling reminded him of when he had slipped the keys of his first luxury car in his pocket. He took a last gulp of coffee, stood up and walked out with a dorkish look on his face.

2

Starkaður kicked himself round in a leather armchair, making the brandy in the glass spin in the opposite direction. Scattered about the room lay DVDs of the James Bond films which he had received as a presentation gift in a metal briefcase from employees of Swiss Bank in Luxembourg. The case had been unusable ever since the special prosecutor engaged a locksmith to pick its lock. He had come around to the view that *Octopussy* was the most memorable of the Bond films, and the best scene in it the one where *007* is out in the forest with only ten minutes to save the world from a nuclear explosion. He hitches a ride, some youths in an open sports car stop and wave him aboard, but when Her Majesty's spy gets close they drive away, laughing, and leave him behind in a billowing cloud of dust. The world has been brought half a minute closer to disaster. Trying to save the world is thankless work. Starkaður was well acquainted with two luxury hotels in the film, both in palaces in Udaipur, India. When he froze the picture, and studied the décor he saw that it had undergone almost no change at all. He felt he had learned something during the time when he had been on the list of the thousand richest people in the world.

What worlds would have come into being if megalomaniacs like the ones in the James Bond films had ruled states, he wondered as he looked at the bronze-coloured liquid. He found it impressive that such men never gave up. In the next film, there was always a new man with a master plan. What was happening to his own plans?

He stopped rotating his armchair. The brandy glass was greasy with garlic oil and did not glow in the flames from the fireplace as it had when he took the cork from the bottle the night before. He went into the kitchen, turned on the hot tap, emptied the glass and let the water run on it. While he washed his hands, he looked out of the window. One night soon after his detention he had spread garbage on the lawn and parked a numberplate-less Volvo sedan next to the one that was in running order, making it look as if it were being kept for spare parts. It stood on a trestle, and lacked its front tyres. The worn out tyres lay in the driveway and a piece of machinery, the purpose of which was obscure to him, rested on the rusty rim of one of them. He remembered that he had called his grandmother late the night before and she had said that reporters contacted her from time to time. She had told them she knew nothing of his whereabouts, only that he planned to take the consequences of his actions, whatever those consequences were. Added that she had passed his house recently and noticed that the tenant was a downright slovenly customer.

'Do you want me to knock on his door and let him know that this won't do? That he'll have to tidy the place up or get out of there?'

'No, Grandma, I owe the man a favour and want him to feel at home. Just let him be.'

Starkaður was once again seated in the armchair with the brandy glass, which now glowed, and the thought that grandma had not known he was in Iceland gave him a sense of security. If she didn't know, then no one did. He didn't even know it himself, he thought to himself, and laughed.

The vertical blinds in the parlour window chopped the shadows on the painting collection like a chef's knives in highly trained hands, and naked branches from the garden wrote constantly between the lines. His eyes hurt with the

19

effort of trying to read the fast-moving script, and he turned the chair a quarter degree.

A metre-tall vase stood on the floor in the dining room, the darkness flowed softly down the opening that reminded him of thrusting African lips he had once kissed at a private club in London. On either side of the vase, the walls were covered with mirrors. Beside it, on an ornamental wooden table, the battered diary Starkaður had secretly taken at Súfistinn lay open. He picked it up and flicked it to the beginning.

March 21, 2009

My apartment is the smallest in town, the size of a caravan. When it's windy it shakes as though it were being blown off the roof of this four-storey building. Here it was once left in the corner under cover of night by lifestyle gypsies who then forgot it. It isn't visible from the street, and people are always very surprised when they think they are on their way up to the attic but then step into my cupboard. While they take off their shoes in the hallway they take in the whole apartment. The visitors invariably relax at once and feel at ease. Here they find shelter from the materialism of modern times. From the bloody war of the status symbols outside.

While I dreamt, my caravan contained the world. Now that the dreams have left me I feel how confined it is. I cannot sleep, and am stuck with myself as I am. And I'm stuck here with the world as if it were a lost, unmarked dog that stares at me, begging. There is no way to avoid the demanding black gaze. If I could only close my own eyes, and disappear.

The last dream I wrote down was number 1139, and it was like most of them then, about leaving my body and flying over distant lands. I didn't know that I had become addicted to inner freedom until I made an emergency landing back in my body and stopped dreaming. That was in New York, a few days after the financial crash. Now I simply observe the weird world we live in, am careful with the few cents that I own and remember the days when I was man enough to sleep with my wife.

She was prone to take me to all kinds of gatherings and introduce me to incredibly real people. Although I called myself a writer without having published anything at the time, all those beautiful faces were kind to me. Because I was her escort and she was happy. I made her happy just by not saying much and allowing myself to find her beautiful both outwardly and inwardly. She could feel it, and needed me not to ask her about the past. Not to make demands about the future. To listen when she talked about herself and not to say a word about me.

I was very glad not to have to say anything. And then she suggested that we get married at the local registry office and tell no one about it until months later. The ordinary wedding kiss was the most beautiful moment of my life. She who would have chosen a white dress, a famous pop singer crooning her favourite tunes for her in a packed church, a crowded dinner, touching and amusing speeches, a band and dancing until the morning, did this for me with unaffected modesty.

My young wife came to join me when she could and slept in my little cabin, though the mattress resting on two sofas placed side by side always subsided into the gap in between. She liked it best here and tried to speculate as little as possible about why that was until she had grown so used to it that it became the basis of her existence. All her great plans began with the same beautiful word: we.

In the shower, while washing off the congealed sweat of sleeplessness, I was conscious that I stood naked on the roof in the middle of town, the city in motion around me. Through the window I heard the meowing of the cat that belongs to the female art teacher on the ground floor. It had apparently been shut out in the rain while she was out walking her dog in Hljómskálagarður Park.

In the mirror, I looked for a moment like a man with a soul. As I had in the past. But I had no memory of the dreams and the expression disappeared. Strange to think that no one around me sees the difference in me after the dreams have left me.

Starkaður looked up and into the mirror, felt that he saw the author writing. He turned the pages of the diary and noticed that in his own way he had begun to write over the author's life: in the middle of the notebook brandy stains had obscured the words, and on the right-hand page cigarette ash formed dark clouds over black sentences.

The book was number 102, and contained 152 closely-written pages. It said that a year before the financial crash, the author had moved to New York with his son Bjartur and wife Hildur, where she took a position at Merrill Lynch. As an official of the Financial Supervisory Authority, Hildur had criticised the policy of the Icelandic banks before and after the mini-crisis of 2006, and been fired thus, but some time later was offered a better paying position than she had ever dreamed of. The couple lived on the eastern edge of

Manhattan's Chinatown with a view of the Brooklyn Bridge, which the author pretended he had never seen; said that they had moved up into heaven, and when he went out in the morning and looked in the direction of their apartment, it had disappeared into the clouds.

Their son attended a private school in the neighbourhood where he immediately settled in and did well. The author only had to escort him to school, pick a café, and write. But after the economic collapse he seemed to have changed in a strange way. He missed the days when they had met in the history department of the University of Iceland, before she took up economics and went to study for an MBA at Reykjavík University. Became so extremely practical. Although in articles he had made fun of the social situation while all went well, the financial crash upset him greatly. He seemed to have lost faith in the value of intellectual life in Iceland. Lost faith in the value of thought there. But even so, he wanted to go home. He stopped being able to sleep with his wife, and described the times of humiliation when he aroused her but could not finish the job. One day in the middle of January he left without saying goodbye. Flew to Iceland to take part in the street protests on Austurvöllur square in the aftermath of the collapse of the banks. Hildur only found out that he was gone when she got a phone call from the boy's school. His father had not come to pick him up.

Despite her being hurt and angry, there was sincere love in her letters, from which he quoted with marked devotion, for the quotations were better written than the rest of the diary. Although they now lived in separate countries, and had done so for a while, nowhere in the densely written pages did the author contemplate divorcing her. But he clearly had pangs of conscience about having thrown in the towel and gone away without letting anyone know, and without arranging for anyone to collect the boy from school.

Starkaður turned the pages until he came across a story that the author had written for Bjartur, when he missed him. It had been prompted by the boy saying on the phone from New York that his father must come home, because otherwise he would never be able to grow up. The handwriting was large, with only a few words in each line, indicating that the text had been scribbled down in a hurry:

Reykjavik, May 14, 2009 - After a phone call with Bjartur in New York.

Once upon a time there was a red-haired boy whose mother allowed to go alone down all the floors of the skyscraper they lived in to play in a big sandbox he had never played in before, but he got lost in the desert, walked and walked until he forgot everything, his games, his school, his friends, his home. Forgot everything except the art of walking until he came to a big river that was half concealed under a sparkling veil of drops that it wore like a mask, impressing the boy so much that he also forgot the art of walking, and came to a halt.

He looked down into the water that was so heavy with sand that his reflection could not rise out of it to greet him. He briefly felt his face. His hands were hot and dry, his cheeks so young that it was appropriate that they were wet.

Through his tears he saw in the mist that on the other side of the river there was a forest, where branches stretched through other branches, flowers displayed themselves with all the colours of the rainbow, feet scraped, kicked and ran, beaks chirruped, sang, pecked and swallowed, and teeth broke in battle or turned black with hot blood. The boy knew that he had to get over to this forest.

He searched for a crossing place, but everywhere the river was too deep and the current too strong, so he fell asleep with the fingers of one hand in the water. When he got up, the search for a crossing continued and lasted until he passed out with fatigue. Such was his existence until he lost track of time. Whenever he closed the green door of his dreams and opened his eyes, he continued to try to get across until he realised that beside this river it was always morning. His mind had been silent but now he heard trumpeted loud and clear:

'If I can't get across I will never grow up!'

He hunkered down on all fours, and wept bitterly. The tears that fell on the palms of his hands were grey as stone. He sat there, letting the sand run between his fingers until they hurt. Suddenly in the distance a stone column began to move and grow bigger. Soon a man emerged from the desert, walking towards him holding out his hand. The boy wondered who it was, until the man spoke:

'Come along, dear son, I'll build you a bridge.'

The man began to build a support for the bridge, and immediately time started to flow again. Years went by, and always the man arrived at the end of his workday to hold the boy's hand from the moment he fell asleep until he woke up.

Once night the boy woke from a dreamless sleep and sensed that his hand was cold, sticking out from under the blanket. No one was holding it. Sleepily he got up and set off in the pitch darkness, following the railing. The deck of the bridge had never been smoother. The coolness from the flowing current was like a maternal caress. He stretched his hand out into the darkness, trusting that his father would take it, felt a sure grip and soon everything was as it ought to be. His father led him to the bed where he lay down, and when a thick wool blanket brushed his cheek, he fell asleep.

*

The next morning was unusual, because when the boy woke up, no one was holding his hand. He rose stiffly, and when the floor shook he found no railing to support himself, only a sharp edge where the floor ended. It was still too dark to see, so he lay back down on the wet floor and waited. Gradually the artistic hands of the morning sun produced a picture of the world; he was trapped on a slippery platform in the middle of the river, a sagging platform that was not attached to anything. From here he could go neither back nor forward. From the unstable platform to the elegant bridge his father had built it was a long way, and the bridge now resembled an abandoned pier in the distance. The boy could not recall sailing between the two structures. And what kind of bridge was it that his father was building? How was he to get across? He heard mighty hammer blows and looked at his father, was startled to see his powerful demeanour. Certainly, he was as friendly as he usually was, but he was also more cheerful, muscular and talkative. The boy understood that during recent years his father had been tired, but now he was full of energy, throwing wriggling fish up onto the deck of the bridge before continuing to extend the platform in the direction of the

26

lush green riverbank that was now so clearly visible.

The boy had crossed over to the wooded slope where busy birds flew between blossom-laden branches. He realised that their singing was often the latest news, arriving through the air at lightning speed. To relax after the effort of the day he went down to the shallows where the murmur of the river drowned all other sounds, and looked into the water. Saw himself with a red beard and scarred face smiling back at him. Looked up and considered the bridge in the distance. Did not yet understand what he saw: in the middle of the bridge there was a big gap that made it impossible for him to go back. He had never crossed this gap, and yet here he was now on the wooded shore. Something had happened in the years out on the river with his father, something he would never understand.

Deep inside he knew that his father had a secret. He longed more than anything to discover what it was, but felt with agonising certainty in his heart that there was only one way to attain it: he must live his life to be as good a man as he possibly could. If he did, the mystery would be revealed to him at the moment of his death.

As Starkaður read the story about the bridge, he felt for the boy who had a father who had given up on life. He himself would no doubt have proved to be a better father. Old girlfriends reappeared in his memory, looked at him with a challenging question. Why had he not had a child with any of them? The author was probably the same age as him, and despite the whining in the pages of the diary he had clearly had a meaningful life with his son. If he himself were lucky enough to have a son, presumably after a long spell in jail, he would be an old man when the boy was grown-up enough to talk to in the way the author did in the story. And then the atmosphere between them would be different. Would his son be able to have any respect for him? Would he be able to respect himself after wearing the stultifying green prison uniform for years on end? He doubted it. But he was convinced that if he had a meaningful life and a good reputation he would at least appreciate it, and be able to give something in return.

If only one could buy honour and a meaningful life. He laughed bitterly to himself. It had begun to dawn on him that reputation grew in the heart of a young child like the seeds of trees. If they were nurtured every day, in the long term they would by far transcend the individual person. One day they would be a magical forest that contemporaries sensed in the presence of the full-grown man. It took a whole lifetime to cultivate a miraculous forest, and once it fell there was not time to cultivate it anew.

'One lies left behind on a charred wasteland, and doesn't understand why nothing remains but the hour of parting.'

He drank a glass of brandy, hung his head and cursed the law of life. Laughed cynically and tried to get rid of the thought that had popped up regularly these last few days. The old obsession had begun to stir, the madness that periodically took over his life and moved him to do the most incredible things. A stubborn voice whispered questions within: Who says that the laws of life cannot go sour and become obsolete like everything else? Doesn't one need to believe that to believe in today?

Angrily he muttered: 'If a good reputation is the basic value of everything, it's the best product on the market. And if it's the best product on the market one can bet that someone has realised that, and has met the demand.'

He fell silent as if he were listening to the sound of the words in his mind. Then he tried to repeat them in a calm, rational tone. With that, the idea sounded like an obvious truth based on sensible marketing. For a while he was almost entranced. Then he snapped off his chains with a cry of triumph, jumped up from his chair and threw his glass of brandy over a plant painting by Eggert Pétursson that hung above the fireplace. The drops that fell into the fire glowed into flame.

'It's impossible that no one has ever grasped this! Some psychiatrist or psychology professor who in middle age has grown tired of the finicky problems of human beings and wants to see real money. Some ambitious fan of James Bond movies who can sell me what I need!'

He clutched his head to maintain focus, through the intoxication.

Now all I need is to understand how a reputation seller thinks, how he markets the product.'

Starkaður felt sure that there were not many people who sold honourable lives to the damned, for then at some point he would have heard them mentioned. It was not simply a matter of providing people with new papers that worked at world's end, like the ones he already had under the name Charles P. Harvey. It was a question of a new self and a good reputation in one's own social circle. It had to be done in secret and in a manner, so specialised that there was little competition. It was even a monopoly. The uniqueness of the enterprise meant that the price was far higher than the lousy two hundred thousand dollars the economist had said was the basic value of a reputation.

He put the cork back in the brandy bottle, returned it to the drinks cabinet. Murmured thoughtfully:

'The merchant of honour certainly exists. But if his activity is secret, how do I get in touch with him?'

3

To begin with the search-words were associated with new life, rebirth, blameless reputation in one's own community, and so on. Starkaður had never bought so much rubbish on the Web, excluding one site after another. He was looking for sites where credit card numbers were required early on and where one needed to pay for all kinds of things to get further into them. Assumed that the people, if there were any, who offered the service he was looking for, let no one get near them unless they were convinced that the person was rolling in money.

By express mail came vitamins to improve concentration and memory, a crystal lamp for recalling dreams, a consciousness frequency inverter disguised as a flower vase and many other self-help aids. He opened very few of the boxes. Gathering in the hallway was a pile of packages he was going to donate the next time neighbourhood kids rang the doorbell asking for stuff for the local raffle. For the first two weeks, he did not touch alcohol and concentrated on the task, answered psychology-related questions and restricted the operation to fifty URLs he thought interesting. When he tired of the subject he had a glassful or two every now and then and imagined that he had sold everything, even the contents of his home, and set off to wander disguised as a pauper. When he looked at the vagabond sites, he saw many interesting options, like how to crash on other people's sofas for several days. After a month, he had made a note of all the likeliest web addresses, and took a day off. He had been offered all kinds of courses and private lessons in this and that, but none of them were what he was looking for. He laughed at the websites and began to wonder about one of them he came across in the first few days that was different from the others, in that the more self-help gear ordered from it, the more expensive it became, while the items themselves diminished in value. He smiled at the brazenness, and realised that ultimately he was paying a fortune for nothing at all. The thought would not leave him alone. Was someone possibly trying to tell him something with this? Was whoever ran the website hinting that ultimately he was selling something invisible, but still more valuable, than merchandise? He decided to look at the site again. After a few days, the seller's posts became more and more interesting, and bore an increasingly strange relation to the product:

The reputation trade is a part of all business. For example, conscious consumers think it shameful to do business with companies that use child labour to keep production costs down. They thereby unconsciously attach a monetary value to their own reputations and those of others.

But what should the monetary value of a reputation be?

The Nobel economics laureate G.S. Buffy calculated that the positive value of a reputation is around two hundred thousand dollars. Its negative value is, however, many times higher. The professor meant that when a company suffers a loss as the result of the actions of a deceitful employee, its value falls more in the short term than when the crisis is due to natural negative changes like an increase in the price of oil. So, it is easiest to price a reputation directly when an employee of a large corporation brings its honour into disrepute and makes its stock fall in just a matter of days, sometimes by millions of dollars.

Only the person who has lost his reputation and wants it restored to be able to enjoy the respect of his own community, understands what this means for the individual. What is such a man ready to shell out to regain his good reputation? And how is he to go about it? If a good reputation takes a long time to grow and flourish, must it then not always be old and well-established? Is it indeed possible to speak of a new reputation? Does the person who wants a new reputation need to acquire an old and good reputation to replace the one he has lost? We have scientific answers to these questions, based on extensive research. If you purchase our report on the matter you will be customer number 401, and will gain access to our unique product.

Without batting an eyelid, Starkaður ordered a copy of the report for $5,500, but when it arrived by mail four days later he did not read a word of it. On the next site, it said that if he bought a meditation DVD of teachings that would set his mind in the spirit of socially trusted individuals of the stature of Nelson Mandela and Mahatma Gandhi, he would be the 203rd customer. The number of customers dwindled rapidly in proportion to a price that soared so steeply it left other sites standing. As far as Starkaður could see, the last product, which was nothing but a broken mirror that had to be pieced together into a glowing gem, had only nineteen registered buyers. He thought it probable that very few people who spent eight million kronur on such finery would receive what the mysterious seller was actually offering. After acquiring the mirror puzzle, he received an email message to the address he had registered for the order, under the pseudonym Goodman:

Mr. Goodman, you are a discerning client. We greatly appreciate it. Perhaps we can do more business in the future. If not, we will refund your expenditure on our products but allow you to enjoy them none the less. You have purchased a ticket in the lottery of life. If you win, we shall send our representative to you. The prize is a new reputation!

Starkaður knew that he had caught someone's attention when he was addressed by name and with respect. But at the same time the ambiguous message let him understand that from now on all he could do was wait. Now the seller would weigh him and measure from afar, and if fortune was with him, approach him. If he saw the sums he had spent on the junk that filled the corridor and lay scattered about the parlour reappear on his bill, he could be sure that the reputation seller did not want to do business, nor did he want anyone to believe they had been swindled and ask what his activities really were.

Starkaður reckoned that in order to track his deposits to bank accounts in foreign tax havens the reputation seller would have to be well connected. But perhaps he needn't do that. The fact that Starkaður had been on a list of the 1,000 richest men in the world, number 791 to be exact, and the fact that he was looking for a new reputation, though it clearly had a certain price, made it possible to guess that he had some capital. If the seller thought he could pay for the service, the next question was how he thought he could trust Starkaður for involvement in activities that were obviously outside all legal frameworks. Having failed such a test in front of the whole country, he was not sure he could pass it now. The seller had some problems, for a man who was looking for a new reputation had obviously lost the trust of his fellow human beings. On the other hand, Starkaður had never broken any laws except financial ones. He was in a grey area, and the reputation seller was doubtless proceeding according to a yardstick of which he knew nothing. Starkaður was optimistic, however, and began to feel better. As though someone he wanted to impress were keeping a constant watch on him. When he realised that he had started to hold his head high, he laughed to himself. If that were so, he had got something for the millions he had thrown away on self-help websites.

Forty-three days and sixteen million kronur went into the search. Yet he regretted neither the time nor the money. Despite everything, he had done something constructive about his affairs. He decided to get himself in better shape and start going out more.

4

Starkaður stood in the doorway, holding his hand over his mouth, as he feared he had bad breath from the previous night's chain-smoking.

'Hello, did I wake you up?'

The woman addressed him in English.

'Er, yes, you did, actually.'

'Such is life! Here I am, then.'

'So it would appear.'

He had no idea who this pushy young woman was. The door opened slowly all the way, and she seemed to take it as an invitation to walk straight in. Without hesitation, she stepped inside, leaving her luggage lying on the steps. In the parlour, she gazed around her:

'This is a much bigger house than I'd expected. Is this the sofa we agreed on?'

Starkaður straightened his dressing gown and tried to smooth his hair as he scratched his head. Had he advertised the contents of his home for sale last night as he had sometimes considered doing? He could not remember, but to be on the safe side he nodded.

'This is like a double bed compared to the one I was dumped on up in Akureyri.'

She took out her mobile phone and showed Starkaður a photograph of a stained sofa:

'When you're a couch-surfer the smallest sofas are the most memorable ones. I'm afraid yours is so big that I'll soon forget it.'

Starkaður felt foolish as he stared guiltily at photos of

old sofas while she thumbed through her memories. There were also some photos from restaurants in Akureyri, and two were of a seabird that a bartender had made for her in cappuccino foam. Had he registered his name on a couch-surfing site one night? He couldn't remember, would have to go through his Sent Mail folder, and see if that explained the disaster. He was tired of looking at phone pictures, and put on an artificial smile, covering his mouth with his hand:

'That's fine by me. You forgetting my sofa, I mean.'

When he saw her on the security camera he had thought she was lost, and had opened the door to give her directions, probably to the bus terminal. Now she had brought her bags inside, and sat on the sofa with her feet under her. Stroked the cushions with her fingertips, the nail polish on her fingers worn.

'Dear, dear sofa, did you miss me? Everything looks like home from here! At last I feel I have a place to stay in Reykjavik.'

Her holdall was covered with the flags of various countries, her jeans patched and re-patched like those of a real globetrotter.

Starkaður reached for the bottle of Camus and was about to rinse the bad taste out of his mouth, but noticed that the interloper was watching him closely. He looked for a glass, but the quiet eyes behind him steered the bottle into the drinks cabinet. There was a crunch of broken glass beneath his slippers, the soles of which stuck to the floor.

'Excuse the mess, I had some colleagues round for, er, cards last night. That's why there are all these pizza boxes, you see. But don't worry, I won. You must be famished after your journey. Wait, I'm sorry, your name escapes me.'

'Rita.'

'Yes, of course, how silly of me. I should have remembered it. The name of a migratory bird, the well-travelled cappuccino species. All you need is the feathers.'

In English, he found it easy to fall into improvisatory patter again, having done it for well over a year in India. Was also reminded of how bored with it he was, and felt ashamed. Wanted to say something that was true, but was already tangled in his own net:

'Well, to tell you the truth I'd quite forgotten that I was expecting you. I've never had a, what do you call it? Sofa bird? Or couch surfer? At least, I don't know what it involves. What did we discuss? Were you planning to stay for a while?'

'We only agreed on a month to begin with.'

Starkaður nearly passed out.

'A month!'

He felt she was looking at him mockingly, and his stomach seemed to be eager to show her the mish-mash of stuff he had been eating in recent days. As inconspicuously as he could, he put his hand over his mouth. If he was not going to throw up, he had to lie down. He wiped the cold sweat from his temples with the sleeve of his dressing gown:

'Listen, Rita, we'd better discuss this later. You'll manage in the kitchen with, er, severity and courage, and you'll find duvets and pillows in any room. Just be careful you don't get lost. If you need to wash bed-linen, or things in your backpack, there's a washer and dryer downstairs. Meanwhile I need to work in my room. I'm under a lot of pressure!'

The woman fetched her backpack and began to spread her belongings around the room. She showed no sign of listening to him. Starkaður grabbed two over-filled ashtrays and placed them on a stack of papers on the night table in the bedroom. Then he swallowed two paracetamol tablets, and, sweating profusely, subsided on top of the crumpled bedclothes. He rolled about groaning for a couple of minutes before falling fast asleep.

It was twilight outside when he woke. He got up, to reassure himself that there was someone in the house. She was sound asleep on her newly found sofa, her hand under her cheek. Her guileless dream-face broke through her sleep, exposing the fact that she was older than she seemed at first sight. Over thirty, he guessed. She seemed too old for the mode of travel she had chosen. Her cell phone blinked on the parlour table like a beacon, on top of an English-language map of the East Fjords. In order, not to wake her, he placed a front door key gently on the phone. He reached for his laptop and some printed sheets, and took them upstairs.

During the next few days he saw little of Rita. She went out early, and he used the time to try to reset his clock and get himself fit again. He used the exercise room in the basement for the first time since his return, and got the sauna going again. Quickly he moved all his things upstairs, and used the kitchen and bathroom there. He found that having her stay in the house was an advantage, because people suspected even less that he was at home. Sometimes when the front door closed downstairs he peeked out through the vertical blinds to observe her walking out through the yard. She was always well dressed, and there was no sign that she might be particularly reckless or mad. Why had she not realised that she had come to the wrong address? Someone must have texted her asking where she was. Starkaður would not have been surprised if she had disappeared one day, and it made him apprehensive.

For the first time in two weeks he put clothes in the washing machine, shopped for groceries, cooked, and smartened up his appearance.

5

Watching him at Súfistinn, Starkaður had an increasing sense that the author inhabited a dimension of his own there. When he went to the service counter he never had to order. On spotting him, until three o'clock the waitresses simply asked: 'Caffè Americano?' He had only to nod. After three the same situation prevailed, except that then the question was: 'Fruit tea?' Starkaður had calculated that the author received a 25% discount on everything he bought, perhaps because of the large number of visitors who came to greet him. Normally the waitresses called out the orders when they were ready, and people came to collect them. Except for the author's orders – the waitresses always brought them to his table. The author rarely had the energy to say thank you, but this seemed not to bother them. If they got an order wrong, they liked to bring him a cake or hot ciabatta rather than throw the food away.

All he did was read, write, listen to the people who sat down beside him, look outwards, away from the world, and simply be. Could there be an easier, and cheaper, way of living a good life?

The author was playing chess with his son, whom he always allowed to win. It was as though he enjoyed letting himself lose. It occurred to Starkaður that this was very similar to what he did when he held discussions with people. As when taking part in a game of chess, he let them apply themselves and cleverly drew out their method of argument. He helped to make sure that they won, and presented them with a sly award that consisted in making them feel important. All those who greeted him did so with a warm smile. As though life had a specially chosen purpose for them. Could death, despite everything, give people pleasure, if it were cooked and prepared the right way? When Starkaður thought about this, he felt that he was one of the guests at the author's table. While father and son played chess, the son told the father the idea for a fantastic tale he was planning to write, and then said:

'Dad, have you ever had this idea?'

'No, never.'

'Strange.'

'Yes.'

'And yet you call yourself an author.'

'That's nonsense, of course.'

'Yes.'

'Dad.'

'Yes.'

'Imagine if I wrote a story and used all the ideas that authors could have, and made them into a book.'

'Yes.'

'Then all the books in the world would have been written.'

Yes, wouldn't that be wonderful?'

Starkaður had established that the author's name was Almar Logi Almarsson, that he had written several novels and collections of essays, and that from time to time he received grants from the Icelandic Authors' Association. On the Internet, it said that his books had been translated into Swedish, German and Faroese. He was always on the margins of the literary world, but because of a few readers who were interested in his work, he kept up with it.

Starkaður doubted that anyone knew much about the author, despite all the books he had published. He believed he knew more about the author than his closest friends, because

41

he had read some of the diaries carefully. Although the author scattered them around with incredible carelessness, no one in his immediate circle seemed to be able to muster the energy to read them. Starkaður rarely saw him review what he had written, or browse through the old diaries. He watched how he stared at an indistinct point outside the world, and reflected to himself that the author was like a theatrical costume and a social mask that he himself should wear for him, and endow with real passion.

The author packed up the chess pieces and let the boy play a game on his laptop, then he picked up his pen and wrote for a while. He replaced the cap on the pen, put the diary on the sofa, took out the pack of Camels, and left the room. Starkaður looked at the red-haired boy. He was absorbed in the game.

Starkaður cast a surreptitious glance at the diary. He fancied that the wet ink lost its lustre and dried as soon as he had read the newly-composed sentences:

April 17, 2010

Hildur and Bjartur are here for the Easter break. Yesterday he went to the cinema with Uncle Silli and his boy. The weather was not too bad, and I took a walk with my beautiful wife out to Skerafjörður.

We came to my childhood home, a tumbledown corrugated iron house which in the old days tended to lean in different directions depending on which way the wind was blowing. In the garden, there were dead, black trees that never changed, no matter what the season. I felt they were clutching at the air in just the same desperate way as when I was a boy. Hildur kissed my hand and asked which room had been mine. I pointed to my old window:

42

'Often in the mornings I would tell my mother I was ill. She always believed me, without ever wondering if I was suffering from a serious illness. After a whole week of saying I was ill I pretended to go to school. I left the house early, hid in the garden and watched my mother take the next bus to work. Then I went back inside and slept until noon. When I woke up, I had to think of something to do.'

'You're still doing that today,' Hildur interjected with a smile.

I sent her a sharp look. She smiled teasingly and her smart designer coat came to life. The mischievous girl whom I have watched since she was a cheerful teenager shone through the precisely calculated colour scheme of the woman of the world.

She was right. Most days I sleep late and then wake up to make myself think of something. Nothing has changed, and yet I have had an entire life in the meantime. The community that existed when I was a boy is gone, but I smuggled my life between the dimensions.

The old corrugated iron houses of my childhood district had almost disappeared behind the clumsy villas as though they were drowning in weeds. But the light and the atmosphere were those of thirty years ago. How is it that the air I breathed as a boy has not carried further and that the shouting of my old buddies still echoes in the back yards?

I put my hand around Hildur's waist, and we paused:

'You see, the woman in this house has always owned a Citroen

43

2CV. This one seems to be brand new out of the box. I wonder where she gets a new car that has long been out of production?'

On the evening walk Hildur got cold, gazed around her at nothing at all and said playfully that damp air was the main enemy of hairstyles. Asked me to touch her hair and feel how it lifted back up when I had laid it on her scalp. The summer's day of my youth had clearly not reached her. We talked between decades, as I described the neighbourhood to her as it really ought to be:

'This house once stood in a wide meadow. A mysterious and sinister tunnel of trees led down to it. I never dared to come this close.'

Smiling, Hildur leaned up towards the house I feared most of all buildings as a boy. Her asking, playful expression told me she wanted me to kiss her.

I don't know why I can't. In some beautiful place our love is unspoiled and has survived all upheavals. I'm sure that she hasn't been involved with another man since I sneaked away. Who else has such a nice family, yet feels relieved when Bjartur's little hand lets go of his at Keflavik airport?

Starkaður looked up from the diary and contemplated the guests. Wondered what the emissary of a reputation seller would look like. The money he had spent on the reputation search on the Web had not yet been refunded, which meant that somewhere out there the reputation seller was probably taking stock of him.

How ought he to behave to appear a responsible client? He thought he should probably look as normal as possible. But how was he to do that? He had to go around like a pathetic loser so as not to be recognised, and could not talk to anyone so lest it become known that he was in Iceland.

After his detention, when photos of him in custody had appeared in all the media, he hoped that the public's thirst for revenge would subside and he would be able to show his face among people again. But when the house had been smeared with red paint for the second time, threats and hate mail sent to his official email address, and he had been jostled on the escalator in the Kringlan shopping centre so that he stumbled and broke his sunglasses, and was booed out of the National Theatre on a premiere night, he knew that the anger was such that if there had not been law and order in the country he would have been burned at the stake.

Starkaður thought it unfair that he could not browse the diary at will, as he was certain he appreciated the author's life better than the author himself. This might be likened to dysfunctional parents with an honest and talented offspring. If they were not to destroy it, it was obviously best that the child should be adopted by people who could nourish his abilities. The author had a perfect life, but was unable to develop it to full bloom.

Starkaður finished his cup of coffee and gazed with irritation at the chatting, laughing people all around him. Felt that as soon as he got home there was nothing but watching movies, drinking, and staring out the window to track the couch-surfer's comings and goings. The day would be at an end when he had finished watching the author. When Bjartur put down his video game and got the key for the toilet from the waitress, Starkaður returned the last diary he had sneaked from the pile and took another. When he got home he lay on the bed with the bottle of Camus and continued reading:

45

December 1, 2009. Window seat.

When I got here after dinner my table was taken, so I am sitting here by the window while I wait for it to be vacant. Outside I see bowed skeletons, black eyes, bruises, and humanity's invisible travelling companion: Death rampant.

How many passers-by would grasp his strong hand and let him guide them like a beloved, if they were able to see him?

The travelling companion's principal admirers, the alcoholics and drug addicts, praise him with a steady lifestyle prelude. An erotic foreplay that leads to the great moment when they are lowered into the grave and at last find a close embrace.

That fellow there with the sunglasses in the twilight has got to the point where he sees the invisible travelling companion by his side at all times. Death helps him to cadge loose change and cigarettes from the sleepwalkers of the healthy life. The collection campaign goes extremely well for him. People empty their pockets quickly, as if they were afraid of being infected by man's eternal suffering, and hurry away. The man in sunglasses is one of the many who tread the slow, and in a way, provocative, suicide dance. The reason being that he simply does not dare to hang himself.

The longing to die is forbidden. Yet it is written on so many faces which drop their gaze when one looks at them, that one may easily imagine a silent mafia among human beings. A dark, secret rule that actively works, word by word, against everyone being constantly cheerful and happy. This is a romantic mafia in search of a flower-bedecked way out, while all the actual exits from life require excess and violence. Excess, to torment oneself with mortification or dissipation, violence against one's family and body.

Is there no quiet escape route out of life's prison?

This much is certain: there is no rational reason for taking one's own life.

It can be said that man is not free to choose life or anything it has to offer unless he can choose death as the alternative. But that intelligent-sounding statement fails, because death cannot be an option.

First, because death is meaningless, and therefore incomprehensible. There can be no rational criteria for choosing the incomprehensible.

Second, because from the moment he signs the covenant of life, man is bound by a navel cord of debt to his parents, friends, and children. Rejection of life can never overcome the rational individual's emotional connection with life.

Therefore, the false option, death, is always a deceit, constructed on bottomless stupidity. And that is why life is a term of imprisonment. The romantic self-pity mafia sits confined in a maximum-security prison, a cramped universe. Since there can be no escape, it uses the time to develop sabotage techniques. The results can be heard in all the trivial and negative phrases that resound here at Súfistinn all the livelong day!

It remains for us to find a complex, considerate and beautiful

47

escape route out of the prison. When that route is discovered, it will be an option for those who choose, and real freedom will come into being. Then I will get down on the floor, locate the secret trapdoor under the table, and crawl through the tunnel into the black freedom of nothingness.

But I am going to start by sneaking over to my table, now that it is finally vacant.

Goodbye, dreadful window seat!

6

The sofa bird had been singing in the house for over a week when she knocked on the upstairs door with a towel round her hair.

Starkaður opened the door, a pair of reading glasses on his nose and Almar's diary open in his hand. He hoped she had come to say goodbye, but she surprised him by asking if he would like to come downstairs and have dinner with her. He cleared his throat and remembered that he hadn't spoken to anyone since his chat with a waitress at Súfistinn two days earlier. Looked at her silently, and emitted another throat-clearing sound.

'I bought a char which I'm going to try to fry with sweet mango and chilli salsa. I had some at Rub 23, the Asian fusion restaurant in Akureyri, and it was terribly good. The dessert is home-baked French chocolate cake with ice cream and cream with coffee and brandy from your cabinet. There's white Jacob's Creek to go with the fish. A bottle each. Nothing expensive, but good. We start around eight.'

She clearly had little need for people to reply to her, for before he knew it she was going down the stairs. He was unclear as to whether they had agreed to eat together that evening but decided to wait and see. When he arrived downstairs he recognised neither the apartment nor Rita. If all the women who travelled about on the sofas of strangers were as domesticated and tidy as this, he ought to get more sofas, he thought. Her eyes were grey and attentive, her pupils small and sharp as industrial diamonds. The expression of her face was perhaps a little too sincere. Her movements were quick and assured, and her cooking indicated that she knew exactly what she was doing. A shudder passed through Starkaður, and he cursed himself for having let a total stranger into his home. He was careful to stick to his dorkish disguise, and pretended to be too shy to look her in the eye for too long. Leaned against the refrigerator and watched her put pine nuts in the salad. Lowered his voice, and said:

'I only rent this place.'

'Oh, really? What's your name, may I ask? I didn't catch it. It all went so quickly, with us. You just disappeared upstairs.'

'Aðalsteinn Svanur. Look here, hmm, Rita, isn't it? Rita. Yes. Perhaps it's best if I put it this way: I wasn't expecting you. Either you've been in touch with the owner, Starkaður Levi, and he agreed to let you sleep on his sofa. Or, well. Or you've quite simply come to the wrong address. Not that it matters to me. You being so good around the house, and all. There's certainly enough room, as you've probably noticed. Though the sofa is perhaps quite disgracefully large, the...'

She took him by surprise with a burst of laughter. He could not make out the tone of her hilarity. Was there sarcasm in it? Or was it admiring?

He suppressed a confident smile that was incompatible with the dorkish disguise. She invited him to sit down, and he accepted with thanks. In the centre of the table she had placed candles of many colours. He picked up the lighter and ran it over them, one by one.

'It's just that I wasn't expecting anyone and so everything was in a mess here when you arrived.'

She sat down, spread a napkin over her knees. Glanced at him.

'Starkaður Levi, was that the name you mentioned?'

'Yes, were you in touch with him before you arrived?'

50

'No. Not at all. But I know the name. I think the woman I stayed with in Akureyri was talking about him. Now I remember. She began talking about him because he was mentioned in the news in connection with the collapse of some bank and the sky-high rates of interest on some kind of loans falling on the public. Is that him?

'That's the man.'

Rita put fish and vegetables on his plate.

'Here you are. Are you in touch with him?'

'Thank you. Who?'

'Your landlord.'

'Starkaður, no. Not many people know where he is at present. Perhaps he's enjoying some freedom before he lands in jail. I just hope he stays away as far as possible for the next few months. Meanwhile I have the house to myself. The fellow owes me money, you know. Money that's quite certainly been lost, even though he's off somewhere sailing his yacht which has a golf course on deck and other refinements. What do I know about the showy lifestyle of these wretched tycoons."

'Exactly. What do we know about people like that. Here, have a drop of Jacob's, the poor man's quality wine.'

She poured him a glass, and raised her own:

'Here's to us two couch-surfers.'

Starkaður forgot his troubles over the food and wine, and his thoughts wandered to the good old days. He could not think of much to say until he was quite tipsy:

'I can tell you this, Rita. Since I moved down from Snaefellsnes my life has been rather dull. My old friend the author Almar Logi Almarsson, who does a lot of his work at Café Súfistinn in the Iða bookstore... have you been there? Yes? Then perhaps you'll have seen him at the table opposite the cake cabinet? No? Anyway, he says that I don't lack a zest

51

for life, ideas and a fine spirit. He, on the other hand, has a wonderful son, Bjartur, whom he sees only rarely when the boy is in Iceland. Then they play a lot of chess at the café. And he has a wife in New York who I think is still attracted to him, but is getting a bit tired of the distance in his expression. All day interesting people sit with him and buy him food and drink. Yet he loathes his life, himself, Icelandic society and window seats in cafés. I have told him many times to look at his way of life and compare it with the existence of anyone else. Especially since the crash. Then he will realise that his existence is the definition of a meaningful and loving life. But he won't listen to me. Any more than if I were a stranger at the next table. In my opinion, Almar's attitude to his own life is a good example of how the offspring of today frequently...'

Starkaður fell silent, as the sentence he had intended to deliver appeared to him like a suspension bridge collapsing before him, and down he went into a deep abyss of meaninglessness. The brandy he had with his coffee after dinner had started him inventing a friendship with a man he did not know at all. Rita's thoughtful eyes were glowing. She seemed to have been listening to him with more attention than he himself. He felt he was back on the islands of Lakshadweep lying to one more weekend woman whom he hoped to land in bed.

Rita seemed to have particularly enjoyed his stories about Almar Logi, but asked no questions about the author. He was relieved. It was best to keep the lies to a minimum. The surest way to do that was to get her to talk about herself, but he did not feel like more conversation. It would lead to lying, even though he said nothing. All his reactions to her words would be the typical reactions of Aðalsteinn Svanur, and he was not in the mood to go on playing the role with any enthusiasm. Rita was no conventional beauty but undeniably very attractive when she threw caution to the winds. Her red wavy hair gleamed in the light from the candles. Through her thin dress the bra could be glimpsed over small, round breasts. Starkaður looked at the clock, felt the evening was over. He fell into the introverted phase, fancied he saw his face get out of practice in responding to the world until he resembled an abandoned farm. She looked at him as though she hoped he was making up an entertaining story. He gave her an expressionless look and heard himself say:

'Has the Reykjavik nightlife held any attraction for you?'

'No, I don't know anyone here. I'm not one for going out on the town alone. Where I come from it's not done for women to do that.'

'How about going out with me?'

'I don't know you, do I?'

'You know my sofa. So how can you say you don't know me? Actually, I can't introduce you to many people... because I'm from the provinces, you see, and haven't gone out much myself. But we could go exploring together. What does the globetrotter say to that?'

Rita did not reply, but disappeared for a while into a room where she could be heard making use of wardrobe and bathroom. Returned twenty minutes later with impeccable lipstick and wearing a red coat that could hardly have emerged so smoothly from her backpack.

*

Outside the B5 bar on Bankastræti Street stood a queue that was based on a complex interplay of physical strength, good

53

looks, fame and tortuous connections with the bouncers. Starkaður found it painful to see his escort get soaked outside a wretched little joint full of affected middle directors. He squeezed his way with excuses through the crowd to the bouncer, took his hand, and on letting it go left a five thousand kroner note in it. Then showed two fingers and nodded in Rita's direction. The bouncer gave him a searching look and whispered to his colleague, who was surreptitiously passing messages to hardened members of the queue. Starkaður was beckoning to Rita to make her way through when he suddenly felt an elbow drive deep into the left side of his stomach. Never before had he cracked a rib, but now it was unmistakable. He saw before him a clenched gloved fist rummaging around in his entrails for the key to a vault. A sense of injustice boiled up within him, but before he could so much as utter an oath, a knee shot up between his thighs. He did not manage to regain his balance, and an iron-hard fist, that seemed to be the size of his face, struck his left temple. For a split second he saw a red sea eagle in flight. Then a shot rang out, and the bird fell rapidly towards the stormy sea.

Starkaður did not know how long he had been unconscious. A girl in a short yellow skirt strode over him, leaving a gob of spit on his jacket as she passed. As soon as it landed, Rita wiped it off his shoulder, and attended to him with a bloodstained cloth. He quickly rose to his feet and was about to shrug it off, but felt pain in his abdomen, and doubled up. On the way he spat blood and swore. He had gone up Skólavörðustígur into Bergstaðastræti, and was opposite the entrance of Steinar's Bookstore when he heard the click of heels behind him, and glanced round. Rita was gazing at him with a look of concern. He leaned against the shop window, and it took him a moment to catch his breath:

'Sorry, Rita. I don't know what that grand reception was all about. I think they probably got the wrong man, and thought I was a drug dealer, or worse.'

He tore a few bloodstained five thousand kronur notes from his pocket and reached them out to her.

'Here, take this and go and enjoy yourself. Then we'll talk tomorrow.'

Rita did not even look at the banknotes.

'Nonsense, Aðalsteinn, I'm seeing you home.'

He hitched up his trousers, which kept dropping, and realised that the belt buckle had broken. While he tried to reassemble the belt, he said:

'Though my party gear needs a bit of attention, you are fragrant and ready for the nightlife. I don't want to ruin the evening for you. You don't owe me anything'

She seemed to consider a reply, but then decided not to say anything. A group of teenagers passed, singing. One of them kicked a bottle away until it broke in the gutter right beside them. The group disappeared around the corner and Rita began rummaging in her holdall. She fished out some old chewing-gum wrappers and receipts which she threw on the pavement. He found it soothing to watch her in her little private holdall world. From a silver box came a cigarette, which she stuck in his mouth and lit. Though it hurt his fractured rib, he inhaled the smoke deeply, took the cigarette out, looked at it as he blew the smoke away as if he expected to see a Red Cross sign on it. Next she handed him a pocket flask, from which he swigged vigorously. While the whisky warmed him, he looked more closely at the flask: it was apparently covered in gold leaf. He realised that, despite their dinner conversation, he knew almost nothing about her.

'Listen, Rita, if the night life is too wild for us poor

squatters, what do you say that we go for a drive instead and look at Snæfellsnes?'

Rita took the flask, and looked shocked.

'You want to tour the countryside in the middle of the night?'

'Why not? You seem to be well prepared. At least, gold and treasures come out of your holdall. We'll just take it with us and we'll be fine.'

'Isn't it pitch dark beyond the city lights?'

'Come on, you can't exactly pretend to be a couch-surfer if a little car trip to Snæfellsnes holds you up.'

Rita did not reply, just continued her slow, rhythmical smoking with a distant look in her eyes. He found that he liked her silences:

'What's more, the sofa at Snæfellsnes is much smaller. So small in fact that it will stand out in the photo collection on your phone.'

On the way he worked hard to make her talk, until she was telling such lengthy stories of her travels that he began to doze off at the wheel. During the stories, he reflected that she was naive, and regretted having travelled out of town with her. The only story he found interesting was her account of how as a child she had moved with her parents from Canada to Europe, and had lived in both Germany and France. So, that when she returned to New York she could work as an interpreter. He had a feeling that she was confused about which parts of her stories were lies and which were not, but he was now too indifferent about her to investigate. To keep himself awake he told several stories about his friend Almar Logi, and then wished he hadn't. He especially regretted having left the Volvo at the garage up in Höfði and switched over to the Porsche SUV he had not used for over a month. Why had he done that? To impress her?

Or to patch up his self-esteem after being beaten like a cur by men whose faces he never saw?

Whatever the answer, none of this had touched her, and he found her increasingly boring to be with. As they sat on rocks on the seashore below the lit-up bungalow he did not even want to look at her, though he felt she was watching him attentively with the gold flask in her hand.

He chain-smoked and enjoyed the plashing of the shore. The painkillers had started to work, and the nightlife excursion now seemed to him like a bad dream. He watched the tide coil around his feet, take hold, stay a little while, let go again. Was glad of the complete halt in their conversation. Her silence was truly first class, and she seemed to have a presence quite different from when she was talking. For a moment, it occurred to him that perhaps people felt about him in the same way. He forgot her, as he began to talk softly to himself:

'In the cool air there can be kisses that creep into one and nurture the will. There's nowhere else where nature caresses you more gently and then a moment later doesn't give a damn about you. Keeps constantly sending this ambiguous message. Nature here is something that won't, even at the last moment, show you love. Yet, when you must part from her, she is like the family you had when you were small but were never able to appreciate until you looked back on it as an adult. Perhaps what she teaches you most is to play a double game, to divide your mind....'

He had been speaking Icelandic, and was startled on being interrupted in English. Rita's voice was suddenly anything but soporific:

'Is a reputation like the waves that play with you as if you were the king of the ocean for a moment? Only in the next breath to leave you in sopping wet shoes in the sand? Like a

57

corpse cast up on the shore? Are you thinking something like that?'

They watched the wavelets display their talents. He was not sure that he had heard correctly or dreamed this. The stone he had been about to throw in the sea just then found its way into his jacket pocket by stealth. He held his breath, intently following the lesson of the plashing sea in its law-governed inspiration. She looked out over the waves that were competing for a chance to seize their share of the moonlight, as if they were licking ice cream. After a long pause, a voice resounded in his head again with metallic clarity:

'It's hard to say how one's reputation is attached to one. How it changes from one moment to another. Who knows what the voices out there are whispering tonight? But this much is certain: a good reputation is so hard to find and is such a valuable commodity that only the soul itself can compare with it. Do I guess your thoughts right, Starkaður Levi? By the way, isn't it more natural that I call you Starkaður Levi, rather than Aðalsteinn Svanur? I mean, since that's your name. Or are we talking here about some Icelandic naming custom that I'll have to learn?'

For a long time Starkaður was reluctant to look up, and followed the movement of each ripple at his ankles with his eyes. He saw the pebbles move and stop alternately, as if each wavelet threw a fateful dice.

'I've grown remarkably used to a name that's different from Starkaður Levi. One's name is really like one of the suits in the wardrobe. Certainly, Starkaður is my favourite garment, yes, but it's up to me to make sure that it doesn't get dirty and threadbare, not to say covered in holes and literally falling apart. Aðalsteinn Svanur is a terrible name, but at least it's better than Charles P. Harvey. Though I sometimes miss Polar

Levi, as the Russians sometimes used to call me when I was there gathering capital for the bank shares. There it did pay to be an ass and not understand what was involved when it came to the question of protection money. Are your disguises usually more stupid than...'

Rita quickly stood up, giving a clear indication that the conversation was over.

'I am much more stupid than my disguises might lead one to believe. Good night, Mr. Polar Levi, the sofa beckons.'

7

While they waited for the flight, Rita had told him that the place where she worked was called The Small Firm and consisted of an inspector, who performed various functions, herself, whom she referred to as "the co-ordinator", and the chief executive, whom they usually called "The Doctor". The firm also did business with contractors in the medical and software industries, for example. The staff were generously paid for specially designated tasks, and they asked no questions about the company's activities as a whole. He had asked for more information, but she had given ambiguous answers. She said that all he needed to know would be explained when they landed in Canada. The company's jet was a Falcon, an older version than the one Starkaður had owned until the summer of 2009, when it was among the assets that were seized by his creditors.

The Small Firm's inspector was a large, burly fellow dressed in a flying suit. He was sunburned, and the ring finger of his left hand bore the white trace of a ring. Triple circles of fatigue around his eyes indicated that he had at least as many children. He introduced himself as "Clark". His sturdy handshake was accompanied by a friendly grin which indicated that he did not expect Starkaður to believe that this was his real name.

Once they were airborne, Rita took care of the catering and put on a romantic comedy which they watched with little interest as they ate. Starkaður guessed that they were New York Jews, and that the plane was most probably on its way to the United States. Some time into the flight he lost track of the time, as he had handed Clark his cell phone and watch at the beginning of the journey, and the curtains in the windows were drawn. Rita was talkative, but as Starkaður did not believe much of what she said, he quickly grew tired of her chatter. He pretended to be interested in her in the hope that while she talked about herself he would indirectly find out more about the Small Firm. After asking her about her girlhood in Germany and France and her years as a poor student in New York, he was finally able to edge closer to the matter on which his mind was focused, and inquire about how she came to know The Doctor. Rita leaned forward over her knees and looked down at her clumsily varnished toenails, stroking her legs as if to check if she needed to shave them. She said she had attended evening classes in psychoanalysis, and had first heard of him through a fellow student. The Doctor was a respected psychoanalyst who had become a well-known theoretician in his field by the time he was forty. Many national celebrities had had sessions with him. He believed that the only way to assess whether the quality of one period in human history was higher than at others was to measure the character of the individuals who shape society at any given time. If the quality of personalities increased, it meant that society had made progress. If it did not, it was a step backwards, no matter what technological progress had been made. Starkaður sensed that she had arrived at the subject that interested her most, because she seemed to have forgotten him, and there was now a meditative gleam of admiration in her eyes:

'He wanted to examine society at its core, which in his view was the psychology of the most ambivalent individuals. I found his ideas fascinating and was eager to meet him. But I could not possibly afford to take private lessons with him, and approached him on the pretext that I was writing a paper

61

on his theories. We soon became good acquaintances and he offered me a few free sessions. I did not realise that this was his way of finding out if I could be trusted. After making a thorough study of my personality, he offered me a job with a small company he was forming. The pay was even better than I would have got had I ever finished my studies.'

'Why do you think he pays so well?'

'I don't know. But as I gradually became familiar with the work I was surprised at what grotesque forms high-flown theories about the relation between self and society could acquire in reality. But such is the difference between life and ideas. Maybe it's precisely the grotesque that keeps my salary high.'

She looked at him and blushed as if she had spoken out of turn. She stood up laughing, patted him on the shoulder and said:

'Anyway, that's the reason I'm your flight attendant now, Starkaður. After the couch-surfing canary comes the flight attendant, remember that. It's very important in the study of disguise.'

'It should be easy to remember, as it's absolutely logical.'

'Would you like to order a dessert from the menu, sir? It's easy to do as there's only one available.'

He accepted the carrot cake and leaned back in his seat while he ate it. He was struggling to understand what she meant when she talked about the grotesque forms that had raised her salary. The obscure rigmarole surrounding the Small Firm made him uneasy, but rather than dwelling on it he decided to relax with the author's diary that he had sneaked at Súfistinn. He felt relief as he imagined the author in his own quiet world at his café table:

December 3, 2009

No matter how much I explain to people how utterly empty our culture is, they always look at me as though I had made a confession of love. I will always be someone people want to have close to them, but without looking me straight in the eye. I will never be able to give everything, as I have so much more to hide than to give. I am a sort of resting place in life on its way somewhere else, an oasis that doesn't turn out to be a mirage until afterwards.

I know that suicide cannot be justified. Rational thought itself is bound to life. Suicide is the definitive leap of faithlessness that I would take were it not for all the people who think that behind my eyes I am producing a gleam of love for everything I see. People think that I am, and take advantage of what they consider me to be. But then they unconsciously perceive that I am only an empty shell and carry on further into the green-leaved, dew-wet reality. Into the so-called life that is constantly passing by, like the cars in the street outside. Life is a mode of public transport from which I once fell while in motion, and now I sit outside the window, stuck in the mirror's reflection. But no one knows it, because I am still smiling and laughing. Ha ha ha... Here inside myself, choking on canned tears, I can't even stop laughing. I'm drowning in raven-black laughter inside my head...

Starkaður followed the blurred hands of sleep away from the diary pages. Enticing laughter drifted from afar.

8

Starkaður woke up, closed the diary and stroked his dry lips. He sensed that the plane was coming in to land, and poured a final shot into the brandy glass. The runway seemed to be on the short side, as the brakes were applied so aggressively that the diary flew over into the seat opposite and brandy blurred the ink on the pages. The curtains in the windows were not drawn until the plane had entered the hangar. The first thing that came into view was a battered Cessna that seemed to have last been used for spraying fertiliser. On his way, out down the staircase, Starkaður looked at it, envisioned a majestic hawk trapped in the grime of earthly life. In the hangar was a yellow motor home, equipped with every convenience for long journeys. As on the plane, the windows in the passenger cabin were covered.

They drove for hours, and it felt as though the destination must be hundreds of miles from the landing site. However, Starkaður thought it just as likely that they were driving around in circles so that he would lose his sense of distance.

He felt like a prisoner, and wondered if Clark or Rita were armed, but had not seen any signs of this. Rita had said that if he changed his mind about the reputation deal and chose not to work with the Small Firm, he would be free to go. He only needed to give them a day's notice, as it would take that long to get him out of the firm's anonymous environment to a neutral zone.

Starkaður had begun to read the diary for the second time when he felt by the movements of the vehicle that they were driving along a bumpy dirt road. Rita cleared her throat on the seat opposite him, pulled down her skirt which had worked up her legs and asked with a yawn if they were there yet. Some time later the vehicle stopped. The rear door opened, letting in birdsong and a scent of flowers. On the ramp Clark offered him a cigarette with a good-natured grin, lit it, and pointed to the main buildings. He explained why they had been built to start with, and what took place in the ones that were still used. Then he took the bags out of the luggage space and told him to follow him towards the guest house. The sky above the wooded hills all round was reflected in the lake below the main building. They walked past the villa, a white, concrete, three-storey house with French windows and a tiled roof. The walls were extensively covered with vines, but where they could be seen there were cracks in the plaster, which was peeling off in places. On the lawn in front of the main entrance there was something that Starkaður thought at first was a superfluous mini golf course but that Clark told him was an old fountain system that had been installed by the previous owners. On the pier, a white and brown coloured yacht lay at its moorings.

During the days that followed he went for long walks in the pinewoods around the estate, accompanied by either Clark or Rita, swam in the lake, watched action movies in the cinema room, used the fitness studio and the library and fished for trout on the pier. The only thing he had to do, though he did not know how it helped the reputation project, was to show up for various kinds of tests twice a day. Rita made him take a personality test, a voice recognition test, an intelligence test, a motion test and a lie detector test that included a question about his expectations of the Small Firm. In the evenings, she took him out horseback riding, and he noticed security cameras here and there around the forest. Some of the cameras were in poor condition and dirty, and he suspected that not all of them worked. After the riding excursions Rita made him help look after the horses. The horses were old, and as the whole estate was dilapidated, Starkaður thought it most probable that the Firm had owned it for some time, but did not use it regularly. It occurred to him that The Doctor might be in the main building, watching them through the cameras that were still working. He mentioned this to Rita, who laughed so hard that he dismissed the idea.

On the fifth day Starkaður looked out of the window and saw a dirty orange Bugatti outside the villa. The doors stood open, straight up in the air, as if the vehicle were picking up its ears, enjoying the exquisite tranquillity of the forest after the monotonous buzz of the motorway. Last time he checked, the Bugatti factory hadn't used orange paint. At one time the owner of the car, which must have been at least fifteen years old, must have had it specially sprayed. Shortly after its arrival, Rita appeared with a note from the master of the house on a silver tray, bidding Starkaður welcome and inviting him to have dinner with him aboard the yacht.

Rita thought they would probably be sailing for two days, and she helped him to carry his things on board.

She had been going to take her leave of him in the dining room, but mindful of what she had said on the plane about what grotesque forms The Doctor's ideas could take in reality, Starkaður now had second thoughts. He asked her to stay with him until dinner and give him a better explanation of the company's activities.

They sat at the bar and ordered drinks from the white-haired barman who stood so still while he served them that Starkaður instinctively cocked his ears for unusual sounds.

66

As he studied the man more closely he felt that his neglect of ear and nose hair indicated a deep lethargy, which explained his stillness. When the man brought the glasses Starkaður saw that he wore a cheap steel ring with glass stones, the raw cut of which showed that it wasn't even a copy of a precious one. Behind the barman, outside the porthole the lake had mostly merged with the shadows of the forest, though moonlight glittered brightly in between. Starkaður felt too ill at ease to be able to think up tactical questions, and asked Rita straight out how the Small Firm had begun.

'It's a long story.'

She glanced at the barman, who gazed at her with complete indifference. He was pouring peanuts into a bowl beside her and was about to return to his place but noticed that she was looking critically at his necktie. He fumbled at it apologetically, but did nothing to improve it. While she was adjusting it for the old man, Starkaður took a sip, and then said:

'Let me hear it.'

Rita said that The Doctor was the moving spirit in all this. When he still had a practice, one of his clients was one of the leading political science professors in the country who had developed ideas about a fairer electoral system. The professor was an example of an individual who introduced new constitutional ideas to society. The Doctor believed that every society is composed of ideas, and so held the professor in great esteem. It therefore came to him as a surprise that secretly, at heart, the professor believed neither that society existed nor that abstract value had any significance. His most ardent desire was to be able to disappear without anyone noticing. Outwardly he was a sought-after lecturer at universities around North America and Europe. But he did not enjoy celebrity. He rather felt that the trust he himself had created buried him even deeper in the mechanical routine of bourgeois life.

'A peculiar problem. Sounds like a description of the lives of most of us.'

Starkaður let the barman refill his glass, and looked at Rita. He saw that his comments received little response, and added:

'Was The Doctor able to help the client with this, this problem...?'

'In his own way, yes. At first he made great efforts to restore the professor's will to live. But then he inclined to the view that he had no right to judge a person sick if that person had contributed more to society than most people and was superior to him in a countless number of ways. He put forward the theory that ultimately a death wish was a natural emotion of individuals who were so responsible that they united with the innermost reality of society and its ideas until society was shaped by their spirit. When people had come to know life to the full, the desire to die into society was the healthiest feeling that could be imagined. A similar feeling could be widely seen described in science and literature, such as Durkheim's concept of anomie, which might then be applied to a real example, like Stefan Zweig. The story of Christ's crucifixion dealt with the same theme, though it was just as clear when not placed in a religious context. However, few people got that far, and so the rule only applied to the elite.

Starkaður had stubbed out his cigarette and begun to use it to draw a picture of a sinking ship in the ashes. Was startled when Rita asked: 'Do you follow me?', and inadvertently blew the ash-picture away.

He pretended to be surprised:

'How could I not? You were talking about a pioneering

68

political science professor.'

'And?'

'And he was receiving treatment by The Doctor because his life had lost all meaning.'

The barman brought a cloth and wiped the ash from the table.

'Right. Well. At the same time as the professor was under analysis The Doctor was giving sessions to one of the richest men in the United States. The man was accused of bribing several presidential advisers and members of Congress in connection with the takeover of a bank chain. This former bank director had graduated from the same university as the political science professor and was short, fat and hairy like him. The main difference was that he had lost his reputation and was full of vital energy.

'At about this time The Doctor was convinced that his ideas about the self, to the study of which he had devoted his career, would never apply to any but an elite, and would therefore not be generally accepted. He also felt that although democracy was the desirable system of government, it blocked the real development of the personality. The reason was that if people begin from the premise that there is law and order out there and they are entitled to something good, they are taken as given something that from a historical point of view is an exception to the rule and cannot serve as the foundation of life. If people deduce from this as a priori, they are less likely to feel that they themselves must give meaning to the sublime values of life against the laws of demolition and will therefore never be truly strong individuals. Instead they will become eternal complainers who behave like fools in the name of the freedom society should provide. Broadly speaking, he had lost faith in modern man. He felt that he had thought his way out of what was considered appropriate for discussion in the academic community, and his interest in it waned. As far as he was concerned, he had acquired sufficient insight into the secrets of the self and society, and realized that he wasn't someone who took existence so much to heart that he was part of its inner core of ideas. He felt that his theories only described the obvious for those few who dared to look at things as they were. The third book of his research on the self was in progress, but he put it aside. From now on, he simply wanted to be among the richest of men and enjoy the best that the world had to offer.'

Rita fell silent and gave the sluggish barman a searching look, as if to see if he had been eavesdropping. He, for his part, held a small bottle of cream, but seemed to have forgotten what he was going to do with it. Rita looked at Starkaður, who appeared to be lost in thought.

'I don't know if, after hearing this story, you can put two and two together, Starkaður.'

With straws, they stirred the cocktails the bartender had brought them, unprompted. During her account of The Doctor's ideas Starkaður had lost the thread, and clearly needed time to reflect:

'No, I've never been any good with small numbers. If you can raise the stakes, we can talk.'

Rita turned up her nose as if she were wasting words on a little boy who had demanded an explanation of matters he was not equipped to understand.

'Anyway, let me finish the story. In the end The Doctor brought together the banker who was full of vitality but had lost his reputation, and the political science professor who was famous, but tired of life. With the agreement of both there came into being a well-respected man full of vital energy.'

Starkaður raised his hand, as if to prevent her from saying more for now.

'A well-respected man came into being, you say. What happened to the other one?

'The other one?'

'Yes.'

To Starkaður's surprise it was not Rita who answered the question, but the barman. His weary expression vanished in a flash as he leaned forward on the bar counter, cleared his throat and said in a gruff, powerful voice;

'His existential dream came true.'

'Existential...?'

Starkaður looked into the barman's deep set eyes uncomprehendingly. The old man raised his hands as a sign that everything was absurd, and said softly:

'He went away, relieved to escape from it all without letting people down.'

9

They had sat drinking at the ship's bar until well after dinner time. Starkaður had begun to doubt that The Doctor would show up, when the old barman joined the discussion. Now the man looked at Rita and gave her a sign that she could make herself useful:

'Rita, how about asking Clark to get started in the kitchen and lending him a hand before you go? I expect our guest is starving.'

It had never occurred to Starkaður that the barman might be The Doctor himself. When Rita had lit the candles and the food had been placed on the table, the man poured white wine into glasses and apologised for not having been able to come sooner. For one thing, he had been busy, and for another there would not have been much point in him arriving before the results of the first tests had been obtained. He said he hoped that Starkaður had enjoyed being on the estate during the last few days and talked about things that needed attention there. Said Rita was very good about making sure that everything went smoothly, and sang her praises:

'But no matter how much she has told you about me, you would never have guessed who I really am. Even if you had it wouldn't have led to anything. Work in the fields of self-improvement and reputation-rehabilitation is such an integral part of the image of society that not only is it invisible, it is so well executed that no one is interested in seeing it. In the last analysis, everyone benefits. So why should they ask questions?'

Starkaður nodded and sipped his white wine. After the day outdoors he was hungry, but it had been such a shock when the barman turned out to be The Doctor that he got stomach cramps and lost his appetite. He could not help staring at the man, and wondered where he knew him from. While he was thinking about this, he took in nothing the Doctor said, until he got his bearings. The Doctor was an older and more refined version of Clark. Yes, he had the same ingratiating grin. He guessed that they were father and son, and imagined that the wife was broader-faced and stronger-looking than the husband. It seemed to him that The Doctor had at one time been dark and handsome like Clark. Now the wrinkles had formed trenches around his face as if it were a mask that could be replaced at any time. Despite his wealth and his need to drive around in the specially sprayed Bugatti, he was not vain enough to have a facelift. Or even just to get rid of his nose hair and have his ears shaved. The ring that had seemed tasteless while Starkaður thought the man was a servant now seemed only a pretence of fakery. Starkaður counted four diamonds, and guessed there were nine of them on the ring. He wondered if the hole indicating that one of them had fallen out had never been filled to enhance the impression of poverty.

He felt completely at a loss for words, and said:

'I don't think it would be hard to track you down, Doctor. I'd just look for the only owner of an orange Bugatti in the U.S.A.'

The Doctor slapped the table and laughed. Then with gusto he ate the fish that Clark had served him and began to rattle off stories about famous people who had lost their honour. One of them dealt with a patriarch of the Rockefeller family who was one of the most hated men in America, a legendary miser during the Great Depression. Advisers told him that the best way to restore his reputation would be to give all the poor people who came his way one dollar. Rockefeller felt uneasy about doing so, until it was pointed out to him that it was by far the cheapest way to gain popularity. The Doctor ended the story by saying that this solution would not be possible in modern Iceland. Then he had the table cleared. Taking a cigar for himself, he handed another to Starkaður without asking, and lit both with the same large match. They blew the smoke over the table in a common cloud. Through the haze The Doctor's thoughtful eyes were dimly visible:

'Has it not occurred to you, Starkaður, to simply apologise to your nation and try to restore your reputation that way? Wouldn't that be much easier? Not to say less expensive?'

Starkaður laughed a forced laugh. He thought for a while and then decided to take the long route in his reply. He recounted the apology he had published in the country's most widely read newspaper on the same day he returned to Iceland after fifteen months of absence. Told of his unsuccessful attempt to integrate into society again. The man listened patiently, with a sceptical look. Then he leaned forward with open palms and said this was all fine and good, it was surely motivated by good intentions. But asked if he had, in all sincerity, done his utmost to be forgiven. If he had put all at stake to make his people believe in his repentance and be able to take him back as a friend and equal.

The reiteration of the question troubled Starkaður. He had not expected that a man who had already fleeced him of several millions for nothing more than a ton of self-help crap, would call his sincerity into doubt and ask the same tiresome questions the reporters had asked in the first months after the crash of the Icelandic banks.

He got up slowly, walked out onto the wooden deck and tried to spot his reflection in the waves. The Doctor followed, puffing his cigar. Since Starkaður apparently did not intend to answer the question, The Doctor quickly put a hand on his shoulder and informed him that he owned the lake, Lake Jordan, as he called it, being fond of old stories. Except for rowing boats the yacht was the only craft allowed to sail on it. He suggested it might be time to get under way, and did not wait for a reply; instead, he signalled to Clark to cast off from their mooring. Starkaður watched the light blue sails draw up and catch the wind. On the pier Rita stood reading her cell phone. She was wearing an old grey seaman's sweater that must have belonged to Clark or The Doctor, as the sleeves were rolled up many times. The hem of a white skirt flapped at her suntanned thighs.

On the opposite shore the light in a small hut was visible. The Doctor said he owned the land around the lake but was content to be able to rent out fishing huts on the beach. If people had access to the lake, his activities here would be less likely to arouse suspicion. He said he owned another, identical, yacht that was berthed in Bridgetown, Barbados.

'My research assistant tells me you also kept a yacht out there at one time.'

Starkaður was still thinking about the troublesome topic of whether he had really tried to gain his nation's forgiveness. Distractedly he replied:

'Rita is right. I had a fully manned yacht there in 2006 and 2007, but only managed to make one proper voyage. We sailed round Cape Horn to Tasmania via French Polynesia. In Tasmania I followed the trail of Jørgen Jørgensen, who was king of Iceland for a summer before he ended up as an outlaw. Like me.'

The Doctor was clearly a keen yachtsman, for there was now a flood of maritime stories. Starkaður listened with one ear, laughed from time to time and drank rum in honour of the general atmosphere of piracy. By the time they sat smoking together on the sun loungers under the starry sky he was quite intoxicated. At last he answered the question The Doctor had brought up earlier in the evening:

'Yes, it was fun, that sailing lark, though quite exhausting. But as to your question, Doctor, about whether I sincerely tried to gain forgiveness in the eyes of the Icelandic people, I would like to tell you a story.

'A hunting colleague of mine at Glitnir, which was one of the three major banks that collapsed in Iceland, went to see a philosophy professor at the University of Iceland after the crash and asked how he could restore his reputation. The answer was simple. The professor said he could only do so by returning to the people all that was theirs.

'Because of the uncertainty about the final outcome, my hunting colleague was not sure that he could follow the professor's advice. Instead, he decided to buy half a reputation by giving away 360 million he had received from the bank as a retirement bonus. Next, he saw fit to settle the matter on the Searchlight program on TV, where he allowed himself to be hauled over the coals without raising a finger to defend himself. In other words, he tried to grovel before the nation. Where do you suppose that got him? Yes, he reaped contempt on top of hatred. Not only from the public, but also from the colleagues who had helped him to turn the economy upside down. We accused him of trying to appear morally more responsible than us, and therefore better than us. I mean, I myself told him that what he had done was an act of hypocritical buffoonery.

'I am certain that he would not have had any more success if he had given away all that he had. Added to which, no sane person gives away hundreds of billions of kronur on such a shaky pretext as national reconciliation and restored reputation unless success is gold-edge guaranteed. And that can never be. When one's reputation is gone there is nothing to do but deny everything, fight to the last drop of blood, hang onto what one has managed to conceal. For one is locked into the system. There will be no forgiveness, especially after the Pope was forced out of the indulgence trade. If a man like me goes broke, he will never recover his wealth, for one cannot become rich without trust, and I won't regain that even if I give away everything and more. Men like me must admit to themselves that they are nothing without the money they raked in.'

Starkaður noticed that his index finger was wagging in the air and pointing firmly at The Doctor. Slowly he put his hand on the table and said with a relaxed smile:

'Or we have to resort to untraditional methods. I suppose that's why I'm out here on your lake, Doctor?'

'Call me Solomon.'

'Solomon what, may I ask?'

'Epstein.'

'Epstein?'

'Yes. At any rate, it's a less dishonest pseudonym than Rita and Clark, don't you think?'

'At least it's Jewish,' Starkaður agreed.

The man refilled Starkaður's glass.

'I've heard your speech before, of course, Starkaður. Actually, you're my seventh client. Don't let my questions make you angry. The shrinks' interest in people is incurable where I'm concerned. I asked to hear how you think about this.'

Starkaður raised his glass slightly, then glanced into the man's eyes, which had an expectant look.

'You mean you think I'm a suitable client?'

Dr. Epstein raised his glass to the same height as his, and said:

'Very much so. We must have this completely out in the open, Mr. Levi. Very much so. You are not mentally ill, though you are unfortunate. We at the Small Firm can't do anything about mental illness. But we may be able to do something about misfortune.'

'Like what?'

Solomon smiled. Then he put his hand to his face, covering it for a moment. When the face returned, it bore an ambiguous expression.

'We offer the best costume for the masquerade of fate.'

They clinked glasses.

'But bear in mind, Starkaður, that we lack the key man. The man on whom the friendly takeover rests, and who is a parallel to the university professor in the story that Rita told earlier. The man who has a real reputation but doesn't know how to appreciate it. That man is often what makes a friendly takeover interesting for me. For he is invariably one of the few human beings who endow life with meaning because he is incapable of doing anything but serving it. If we don't find him, as has happened to the Small Firm a dozen times before, nothing will come of this for us old-fashioned businessmen, who are all traditionalists, of course. Then I shall have to repay all the money you've put into the process, and hope that you will simply look on your stay out here in the country as a convenient vacation.'

'Do you have any idea who he might be? The key man, I mean?'

'Yes and no. The medieval alchemists, who did a lot of work on the sublimation of the self, said that all things conceal their opposites. It means that if such a person exists he is already present in your life. Rita has an idea who this may be, and is going to go and check certain things.'

Solomon put down his glass, and gave a weary groan as he tried to straighten his back:

'Now we must trust her for a few days and see if our winds are blowing in the same direction. But tomorrow we shall see if we are man enough to catch our own food. I have shotguns on board, and trust that you enjoy hunting.'

The Doctor gave him a boyish wink, stood up, and Starkaður got up, too. He guessed that when the man was standing straight he measured over six foot two. When his back was bent, they were roughly the same height. They bade each other good night and Starkaður watched him vanish down the spiral staircase.

10

Rita had begun by writing to Almar Logi and introducing herself as assistant editor at a New York publishing house. She said that they would like him to come and give a reading at a little evening they organised once a month at the Trust Coffee Shop in Greenwich Village. After the reading, she hoped they could talk some more about the ideas in his novel *Bernhard Zero*, the ideas about being nothing, which she found so fascinating. It seemed that in a world of narcissism where everyone wanted to expand until their ego was the size of Los Angeles, he preferred to dissolve and disappear. Almar Logi replied that he would consider the offer, if they paid for his travel and accommodation. He was broke. Said he had lived in New York for over a year but never liked it. Hildur, his wife, still lived there, and he was afraid she would attend the reading with their son. Although he loved them, he would find it hard to feel at ease in the discussion after the reading if they were there. To tell the truth, their marriage had reached a stage that it would be more at home in a novel than in reality. If Rita wanted everything to go smoothly it would be best if she spoke to his wife first and prepared her for the event.

Almar did not expect to hear any more from her, and was surprised when he received the flight ticket in the mail. Rita also promised to talk to his wife, as it suited her well. If the friendly takeover process were to succeed, they needed the most accurate information about the reputation donor. If Hildur was approached correctly, there were few people who had a more precise insight into the author's character than her.

The two women met on a sunny day at the Imagine

mosaic in the middle of the Strawberry Fields Memorial in Central Park. Rita introduced herself as an editor who was interested in publishing a book by Almar Logi. He was an introverted and complex personality, something fashionable in the circles at which the publishing house aimed its books.

'I'm glad that it's fashionable somewhere,' Hildur said, cutting her off. The circular mosaic was making her dizzy, so they found a bench and sat down.

Rita said she was sorry if it all seemed rather sudden. She had been in contact with Almar but wanted to ask her more about him as the publishing house made a point of obtaining the best possible knowledge of their authors and their backgrounds. She was going to write an introductory article about him for the publishing house's magazine. If Hildur cared to, she could read the correspondence that had passed between them.

Rita had had Hildur under surveillance for several days, and when they met she dressed in clothes that were similar to hers in order to make it easier to gain her trust. Although Hildur smiled with her lips as she browsed through the printed-out email messages from Almar, her eyes seemed to look for anything that might be amiss in Rita's behaviour. Dr. Epstein had been emphatic that the boy should not witness the conversations about Almar, so she had brought along a kite for him to ensure that they were left in peace. Hildur had a Japanese nanny who looked after Bjartur while they walked about the garden. She ran laughing with the boy on the lawn and helped him to fly the kite and catch it, in turns. After chatting about clothes, they discussed elementary schools in Manhattan, but then Rita asked if it was true that Almar Logi had lived in the city for a time.

'He never felt at home in New York. But perhaps

that will change if he's published here. Then he may be able
to connect with other authors and begin to settle in. It's very
hard to answer Bjartur's endless questions about his father. He
doesn't understand why his father suddenly disappeared. If
you can help me bring him home, I would be very grateful.'

At last not only Hildur's lips seemed to show goodwill,
but also her eyes. Rita put her hand on the back of hers, said
that she could not promise anything in that regard. They
were only aiming to publish a limited paperback edition of
Bernhard Zero. But she would do her best to put him in touch
with people in the business.

Rita looked on admiringly as Bjartur played with his
black crow kite, until he drove a flock of pigeons away from
an elderly couple of Asian extraction who had been feeding
them. The pigeons fluttered into the air with such force that the
old lady dropped her bag of birdseed on the ground. Bjartur
laughed fit to burst, but then went over to them together with
his nanny Mitsuko, apologised and helped to gather the seed
and return it to the bag. Soon he was sitting with them, eating
an ice cream they bought him and chatting with the old man,
Mitsuko acting as interpreter. Rita praised the boy's good
English and his care for the environment. She asked Hildur if
Almar Logi was as fearless and full of high spirits. Hildur said
that sometimes in the past he had been:

'But actually, dreams are his speciality. He sometimes
talked about having got his pilot license in dreams. Said they
were his best education. Each night he dreamed that he left
his body and flew around the world, inspecting it. After the
financial crash this changed. He stopped remembering his
dreams, and that seems to have created an undefined longing
within him. His contact with reality was through the world
of ideas. But when he lost faith in the intellectual ability of

Icelandic society he lost what little faith in reality he had. Lost confidence that he was talking to any intelligent person in his works. Now he is stuck in a strange void I can't get into. I don't know what he is writing, if anything. It's not like when we were studying history and I sometimes read his diaries before I went to sleep.'

Hildur spoke in a neutral tone while she struggled with an ice cream wafer that Bjartur's aged friends had brought her but that clearly did not interest her. Rita felt that Hildur was talking about something that was dear to her heart, and looked at her with understanding.

'He never understood why I took up economics after we finished history. The fact was that after I had left the nest I couldn't let my parents support us indefinitely, and I didn't think poverty was romantic. He also wasn't supportive when I signed up for the MBA programme at the University of Reykjavik. He called it drama college. Said that economics was a religion and people were simply using the MBA programme to build up a inspectorial aura for themselves. We lived in his little garret, which he always said he was going to extend across the whole roof as soon as he could afford it. He wouldn't let me pay for the extension when I had enough money for it. When we finally got enough space for us both here in Chinatown, he couldn't deny that it was comfortable. All he had to do was to take Bjartur to school in the morning, and fetch him back in the afternoon. He didn't even have to spend much time with him at home, as Mitsuko was always available. He could wander around Manhattan and write in cafés or at home in the study where there's access out to the balcony through a glass pavilion. Isn't that the dream of all writers? After I got a job at Merrill Lynch we didn't have to worry about money. I love him, even though he's never more than half in this world. But I couldn't follow him back to Iceland after he disappeared. It was simply too much. It's not so easy for me to get a job in Iceland now, I can tell you. I don't want to become unemployed again like after my sacking from the FSA. I have more than enough direct debits, and some of them are in both our names. If I stop paying the bills he'll end up with even more money trouble than he's in already.'

They watched Bjartur and the old couple feed the pigeons. With the old man's help Bjartur learned how to lure the pigeons so close that he could touch them. Rita asked Hildur what her job in New York involved.

'Right now? Iceland is after me. I'm providing evidence for the prosecution of some of the Icelandic bankers who landed the country in shit. Have you heard about all that?'

'No, except for a mention in the *New York Times*, I seem to remember. Wasn't one of them called Starkaður, or something?'

'Levi?'

'Possibly.'

Yes, we're exploring his relationships with various clients and trying to trace the path of at least some of the money around the world. It's amazing that this douchebag could make off with funds that the Icelandic state will end up having to recover at sky-high rates of interest. He clearly knew where things were going right from early 2007, so he had nearly two years to get the money out and rob the nation. Nearly two years! You can't imagine how much money he has. I doubt that much of it will ever be seen again. Meanwhile, thousands of people sit at home on a bonfire of debt that is steadily heating up. If he gets less than eight years I shall be profoundly disappointed. The damage that he caused the nation and its reputation can be compared to the results of a heavy psychological bombing of Reykjavik, especially after the British classified us with terrorists. While we're dabbling in his business affairs he is off no one knows where, and spending the nation's money on God knows what nonsense. Sorry, Rita, I expect you can hear that this is rather near the bone for me. But at least I'm able to talk about it without being embarrassed, unlike Almar.'

Bjartur had said goodbye to his new friends and was starting to talk about going home when Hildur whispered to Rita:

'If I'm allowed to come to the reading I promise to wait outside while the discussion is taking place. But you must see to it that we go out together somewhere afterwards.'

11

Rita met Almar Logi at Kennedy airport at three in the afternoon on May 14. The reading was due to start at nine the following evening. All Almar had with him was the clothes he was wearing, and a large quantity of old diaries.

When he had checked into the hotel in Greenwich Village and lay on the bed with the TV remote, he stumbled across the hotel's erotic channel. He watched two women doing nice things to each other while dressed in special black leather costumes, but was left unmoved. Back came memories of when he had first arrived in New York with Hildur, when she was settling into her job at Merrill Lynch. Bjartur was back in Iceland with his parents-in-law, and he and Hildur enjoyed the city life. Almar put down the remote, reached into his book bag, took out a diary that was two and a half years old, and with a sure hand turned the pages until he found his place. After blowing a way what seemed to be cigar ash he read:

Oct. 7, 2007

Every day Hildur and I watch the erotic channels at the hotel, something we haven't done before. A bit tipsy after a good dinner on the first night she turned them on to be scandalized, but then I noticed that she was looking over my shoulder when we had sex, at the lively display. This new television stuff has had an unusual effect on us because yesterday we went to the sex museum on Sixth Avenue. In the downstairs part of the museum she bought a dice with sex commands written on each side and said I should choose something she should buy. I chose sexy latex panties with a little pocket for the white remote controlled vibrator. She refused to put them on, let alone wear them on the street, but when I managed to trick her into it, we had a lot of fun. She looked dignified in her grey suit and that made the game even more enjoyable. She never knew when I was going to turn on "Knut, the shivery little polar bear cub", as I called him.

When I turned on Knut he began to shiver from the cold, and Foxy Hildur, who jerked about with an attractive curve in her back, began to heat him up. Eventually she became red and sweaty. Then Knut could heat up again and relax so I could turn him off. When I had teased her for three hours all over town, she demanded that we go back to the hotel, where she tore my clothes off.

Afterwards, she said that although he was nice, Knut was not half as good as me. I pointed out that it was because the remote control that operated me was located in her forehead.

It's strange how relaxed we were. Today we haven't mentioned Knut once. Except indirectly. I told her that I had had an idea for a sex aid for tourists that could be sold by cell phone manufacturers. The way the device worked was by couples connecting remote controls to their phones. The woman wore a vibrator whose speed the man could control through his phone, and he wore the self-pleasure device we saw at the museum, which she controlled through her phone. This way, people who were travelling could at least have some kind of sex life in the evenings when they were in their hotel rooms far away from their partners. Foxy Hildur nodded as she always does unconsciously when I'm talking what she calls "curly hair talk". In the end, she told me to take out a patent on the device, and continued to concentrate on reading the menu of one of the best restaurants in town.

We are sitting on a waterfront bench in Battery Park. The Statue of Liberty seems to be hailing a water taxi in the distance. I am writing with the splendid fountain pen she gave me (to judge by its price she must have decided to take the job here at Merrill Lynch, though we have not discussed it) and she bought this colourful diary at MOMA. If I know her at all, she will probably find an extremely expensive restaurant for tonight. Then Knut will come with us! Something for both of us, I will say if she objects.

Yes, some day's things go just right. Then the shoes in the shop windows are fine, but the shoes on one's feet are finer. Then the air is fresh even though the traffic around one may be blaring like an out-of-tune brass band. Then the woman beside one is wonderfully exotic and mysterious though one knows all her latest secrets.

When the next day Rita came to fetch Almar at the hotel, he had not left it since checking in. She brought with her a chapter from *Bernhard Zero* which she had had translated for the reading. As he ran his eyes over the sheets of paper on his way up Hudson Street in the direction of the Trust, he nearly got run over by the traffic, until Rita took him by the arm and guided him. She said Hildur had left Bjartur with the nanny and would be at the reading, but would wait for them at a nearby bar while the discussion was taking place.

The reading was rather better attended than Almar had hoped, and people showed the kind of interest in his book that he had never experienced at home. A dignified middle-aged man with a yellow silk scarf, who was a television critic, Rita whispered to him, asked why Almar Logi had written a novel about the Devil coming to Iceland with the aim of begetting a child to sacrifice to God. Almar said that the story of the Devil who goes to Iceland, becomes rich by sacrificing the soul of an old man, and then plans to win God's love by sacrificing his child, was a description of Iceland in 2007, as he perceived it. This had not been a fantasy, but reality, as it later transpired. When the critic asked how this idea had been received while all was going well in Iceland, he said that it had not been received at all:

'There is no intellectual life in Iceland. That's to say, there is no one who can read the existential meaning of a literary work and place it in a cultural context. Therefore, no one understood what I was saying. There was no sense in writing this story rather than any other. But if there had been some sort of dialogue about the book, it would have become apparent that it was a stocktaking of the situation.'

Some of those present talked about the novel's connection with the events in Iceland at the time of the financial crash, but Rita directed her question, based on Almar's assertion that there was no intellectual life in Iceland, to the characterization in *Bernhard Zero*.

'Is it true, Almar, that in your book you describe the antimatter of human life, a kind of anti-character who is actually nothing?'

Almar leaned close to the microphone and, taking a deep breath, said:

'Yes, nothing.'

The word 'nothing' crackled in the loudspeakers and echoed through the air. Scattered laughter came from the back rows, but the author did not change his expression. Rita, clad in a black polo neck sweater, with shiny black nail polish, fingered some handwritten notes that featured coloured highlighting, then cast a glance at the pages before going on:

'You seem to bring it on in a truly inward way. As far as I have understood the text with the help of the translator, it is based on your own self-examination, drawn from your diaries and dreams. That is exciting. A sincere desire to vanish is unusual in our modern age. In a world of egoists, you don't want to be in the spotlight but would rather disappear into the woods, into the shadows, into the flow of life that constantly takes new forms. You say that your civilization does not exist, and in your book, you portray a man who is nothing. By that do you mean that you want to merge with your community, vanish into it? Indeed, could you have created the book's main character if that were not the case?'

Almar was not used to answering well-founded questions about what he was really getting at with his books. To gain time, he asked for more water. He quenched his thirst slowly, cleared his throat and said:

'I don't know how much one should say in public about one's innermost desires, Rita. But it is true that it's hard to create a character like the main protagonist in *Bernhard Zero* if one doesn't have an inside knowledge of his experience in oneself. For example, I can name one theme in the book that is based on my own feelings. In the novel, I talk about sacrificing my child. Before I left my wife and son who were living right here in New York I had thought about it for a long time. In leaving, it seemed to me that in a way I would be sacrificing my son, because I was sacrificing the time I would otherwise be with him. And I felt I was really doing it for nothing. I didn't understand why I had to go back to the country in which I had no faith. Leaving merely said that I was being drawn towards nothing. As if I were at home anywhere but with my son.'

'But how deep is the feeling?' Rita persevered, waving her notebook as if it were evidence. 'Are you, in the last analysis, merely describing the non-being of mankind because of your own insipidity? And because of your lack of words that truly capture existence as it is? Or are you so deep that the void itself speaks clearly through you? Do we hear the sincere, deodorising tone of nothingness in your voice when you express yourself?'

Almar Logi looked as though he was not sure that he had heard correctly. He scratched his beard and grinned.

The silence in the room hung by its fingernails from the spotlights that were directed at him, and made his throat dry.

'Well, I'm not sure if the naked void uses me as its representative. Perhaps you need to tell me, Rita. At least, I don't know what to say. If it's so, then I think you are very enthusiastic about finding a way for the void to enter your mother tongue. Aren't you afraid of getting infected when you read the void, of being sucked into meaninglessness, and vanishing?'

After the discussion, which was protracted because of questions from the floor, Almar and Rita were an hour late in reaching the bar to meet Hildur, who, with burning cheeks, had used a bottle of wine as a timer:

'You're three glasses late!'

Rita seemed unsure whether to go or stay. She said that the book publicity event had gone better than expected, and had delayed them, she ought to give the two of them a chance to catch up and chat. With one voice, they asked her to wait, and after she had called several restaurants and found a good one that was still open, she invited them to dinner on behalf of the publishers. Over dinner, Hildur asked for news of friends at home and Almar inquired about Bjartur's social life and how Hildur was getting on at work. At the bar Hildur ordered one glass of wine after another. They were well acquainted with the wine rack and the cocktail list when she turned to Rita:

'Of course, I should have left him long ago, you can hear how humourless he can be. I don't know why I put up with him and don't just ask for a divorce. He could have slept with lots of women since he ran off. Perhaps it's because we have such a beautiful story, and I know in my heart that he's faithful to me. Look at him. Do you think he's been sleeping with someone else? I don't. He's turned into a monk and I into a nun, I tell you, and yet we are not particularly religious people. Do you know why I don't think he's up to anything behind my back? Because when it comes down to it, he's a coward. He doesn't want to be with his family, but he also doesn't dare to leave it completely. During his last month's here in the city he stopped sleeping with me, no matter what I tried with him. But he's not up to anything behind my back because he doesn't want to have to lie to Bjartur in the future. He's here and he's not here. Now he is probably trying to decide whether to go home with me and put an end to this long spell of nonsense. At the same time, he is wondering whether to try to get you into bed tonight and end the marriage. Trust me, I know him. His intelligent silence is composed of nothing but such fantasies. But you know what? I don't think he will do either. He can do anything he wants. He can get himself right out of this fix, he's no fool. But at some point, after the crash he froze, and now he's this silent waxwork of himself.'

Hildur stood up and excused herself, said she needed to go to the toilet. Half an hour later, Almar received a message from her in which she said that while her skirt was around her ankles she could not remember what she had been saying for the past half hour. She had gone straight out to the taxi while she could still remember her own address. Bade them good night and wished them a lot of fun.

Rita and the author drank in silence. Then she returned to the matter of the publication of *Bernhard Zero*. There would be a print run of only two thousand copies of a special collectors' edition for people who enjoyed reading different writing from distant parts of the world. The book would be available in one or two shops and reviewed in some magazines. If it did well, they would consider a paperback reprint in larger quantities. However, this happened only very rarely.

'But I'm interested in your personality, Almar Logi. Would you really like to just disappear from life, if it were possible?'

'I'm doing pretty well at that as it is. Unless there is indoor fog in this city, which would not surprise me.'

'How about we take this up to your room? As a special service from the firm. I could even tuck you in and read to you.'

'Read what?'

'Well, something you'd enjoy. Something soothing.'

Almar looked thoughtfully at her dark red lips: in the evening light, they were the same colour as her hair. Was she making fun of him? Her pupils were large and shiny, but her forehead creased. It occurred to him that she was sober. He tried to concentrate.

'Thanks for the kind offer, but no.'

They watched a grey-haired couple flirting at the next table until the gentleman asked the lady to dance. Almar spoke again:

'But since you're asking about this again, this desire to

disappear, then I can answer you in confidence. I didn't want to say anything in front of the audience in the coffee shop. It's better to let potential readers work out for themselves what my views are and what is fiction. But between us, I don't believe that society exists, I don't believe it's possible to understand historical context, I don't believe it's possible to control society except to a limited extent, and that is certainly not happening in the land of my birth. My homeland is a society based entirely on imitation and reaction. When it comes down to it, the people are devoid of principle and share the same values as those who robbed them, except that the robbers are slightly less dishonest, because they at least know what they believe in and admit it without shame. I don't believe that thought in my language is of any value, because the social environment is unable to react to internal thought, it is not cut out for that. I don't believe that there's a self-grown culture in my country, and so I am the offspring of nothing. If I could escape from the clutches of existence without hurting anyone, I would do so, at peace with men and mice. But it's probably not an option.'

'May I quote you on that?'

'What?'

'That if you could escape the clutches of existence you would do so, at peace with men and mice.'

'As far as I am concerned you may do as you like, Rita. That's to say, as long as you leave the mouse out of the example. Like in *All Men Are Mortal*, where the mouse had done nothing wrong and deserved neither to live forever nor to disappear. But whatever you do with the oft-mentioned mouse, I prefer that you begin by refilling my glass.'

Rita emptied the bottle into the glasses. When she spoke her lips glowed with wine:

'If you want to find the beautiful way out of life, the

way that would not even produce a single tear from a family member, no shame, but on the contrary a proud smile at your vitality and your success, no matter how paradoxical it sounds, then that way exists. I could take your hand and lead you to the door. Even kiss you farewell.'

She smiled teasingly as she played footsie with him. Almar was embarrassed, and loosened his tie. His hands squirmed on the table in heated closeness to hers. It was as if he could not decide whether he should take them and hold onto them as a source of strength or grasp them as the one in authority, and lead her away with him. After draining his glass, he calmed down and sat with his hands in his lap.

'You talk like a guardian angel, Rita. If I were not the pathetic loser my wife mentioned earlier, I would invite you up to my room. But I'm afraid I need to sleep. The dream world is unfortunately the only thing available to me, as your talk has become nothing but empty words. Perhaps I will get the long-awaited letter of meaning from the postman of sleep.'

Rita looked inward, laughed, seemingly at her own thoughts:

'Almar from Iceland: you have never dreamed anything like the reality that I can reveal to you tonight.'

She took the bill and led Almar outside into what he thought was a taxi. Clark opened the door for them. In the back seat Almar soon dozed off, leaning against Rita. She reached for his phone and hotel room key-card. Spread a blanket over him and smoothed his hair so that it fell over his eyes. Before they drove northwest out of the city, they stopped at his hotel, fetched his luggage, and Rita asked for the bill. She cast her eyes briefly over it and asked the young clerk:

'What's this item?'

'Television.'

'Isn't it included?'

'No, not adult TV, it has to be paid for separately.'

Rita shook her head and handed the man some loose change:

'Men are idiots.'

'Yes, ma'am.'

12

Almar Logi woke up with a cough in a bright, spacious room he did not recognise and began by shielding his eyes. On the bedside table, someone had placed four useful items: a pair of sunglasses, cigarettes and painkillers along with a glass of water. The author was soon sitting up in the ornately carved bed, wearing blue sunglasses and holding the empty blue tumbler he used as an ashtray, blowing the smoke out into the room. On the walls were paintings of twins, or doubles, he found it hard to tell which. One of them had fallen off his bike and was crying, while the other was picking his up, laughing. One was falling asleep, exhausted, while the other awoke from a pleasant dream. In one of the paintings a gloomy clown stepped into a human-sized egg, while his smiling double cheerfully broke out of another part of it.

While he finished his cigarette, Almar Logi stared at the dismal clown, trying unsuccessfully to remember who he reminded him of.

Outside the window he thought he heard the neigh of a horse. He looked out, with the cigarette stub between his fingers. In the courtyard Rita sat on horseback with a whip in her hand and the tension mark of a riding helmet on her wet forehead. Her sweaty locks were dark, but otherwise her hair was fiery red in the morning sun, and billowed in the breeze. She waved to him. Almar opened the window and waved back.

'I see you've found the cigarettes,' she called. 'If you look in the cupboard you'll find the diaries. Actually, I took the liberty of buying you socks and underwear, as I didn't find any clothes. Hope I made the right choice.'

'Great. Good to hear it, Rita. But what happened to my phone? And perhaps even more, what happened to my hotel, and, er, New York?'

She laughed until the horse became restless, and joined in with a neigh.

'Get dressed and come on down, we'll meet at the pier. I'm going to introduce you to my friend The Doctor, who owns the place. Don't you think it's beautiful here?'

Almar contemplated the forest-covered mountains around the lake.

'Yes, very. But what is this place?'

'What is it? Where you are is a beautiful dream of a place. Doesn't the answer lie in its beauty? But perhaps that makes no difference to a man who wants to be nowhere. Shall we just say that we're in Ginnungagap?'

Almar smiled back at her, but when Rita had led the horse back into the stables his expression stiffened. Had he forgotten something from the previous night? Naked in the bathroom, he could detect no woman-smells on himself, and felt certain that he had not slept with her. After showering, shaving and dressing, he went out and walked down to the lake. He dipped his hand in the water and let a few drops trickle under his shirt sleeve. Then he gripped his wrist as though the liquid was spurting blood. At the pier lay the *Alba Rosa*, a hundred and twenty-foot luxury yacht. A weather-beaten elderly man in a white, oil-stained peaked cap was leaning over the rail, watching him with watery blue eyes as he smoked a cigar. Almar Logi walked out along the rotten timbers of the quay and took a better look at the vessel. The man had a significant look, as though he were pleased at having penetrated other people's secrets. He blew out a plume of smoke, and said:

'If I could escape from the claws of existence without hurting anyone, I would gladly do so.'

Almar thought he recognised the words, and scratched his forehead.

'Sorry, but who was it who said that? It was some famous author, wasn't it?

'Or just a drunk author.'

Glimmers of the previous night returned to Almar.

'You must be The Doctor, Rita's friend. Do you sail across the water with the souls of the dead?'

'You could say that. But actually, I sail in both directions. I ferry those who want to leave the kingdom of the living over to the kingdom of the dead, and I ferry those who want to leave the kingdom of the dead over to the kingdom of the living. They meet halfway and exchange the passwords of their phones.'

'You could have done a lot for Gilgamesh in his search for Enkidu.'

'I wouldn't go that far. I have no cure for the basic and universal split between natural man and civilised man. The problem that Gilgamesh and Enkidu faced. The cases that I work with are more specific.'

Over the rail The Doctor handed the author a bottle of beer, introduced himself as Dr. Epstein and offered him a tour of the yacht. He said that the mainsail mast rose more than twenty metres above the waterline, and all the sails were well over two hundred metres square. There were five cabins, with berths for twenty people, two engines that drove two propellers, and a bow thruster to facilitate control in narrow harbours. He showed how the air conditioning and heating system worked, and for a long time patted the machine that made fresh water from sea water. The pictures on board were of twins, or doubles like the ones in Almar's bedroom in the villa. After the tour of inspection, they mostly discussed the transmutation of souls in literature until The Doctor invited him to dinner together with Rita.

*

Starkaður followed the conversations of Solomon and Almar Logi on a screen in the cinema room. The Doctor was of the view that if the difficult takeover process was to succeed, he would have to scrutinise the behaviour and reactions of the reputation donor from the first moment that he came to the project. Clark had cleared the table and began to demonstrate his mastery of mixing cocktails at the bar. Almar Logi pointed at The Doctor with the gold fountain pen he had taken from his jacket pocket and said, in a slightly slurred voice:

'Are you saying that it's possible to walk out of this broken home, the world, without hurting anyone, or leaving scars on those one has left behind?'

'Not only that. I'm saying that if someone wants to turn his back on life, but doesn't do it, he is the bane of the lives of all those around him. His mind is a black hole that causes a cold draught from meaninglessness. That's why a person like that can improve his existence by giving the torch of life to others who long to carry it. That way he improves his own life and the lives of all those near to him.'

'After he's gone?'

'Exactly.'

Almar Logi toyed with the fountain pen. He removed the cap and put the nib into his cocktail, stirred the liquid sceptically, and shook his head. Ink oozed out, darkening the drink's colour.

'Talking of leaving and not leaving, am I a prisoner in this place, whatever it's called?'

'Ginnungagap,' Rita interjected, tilting her head and brushing her hair away from her forehead.

Dr. Epstein literally gave her the floor by signalling to her to continue. She looked at him as if she were deciding what she might be allowed to say. When he nodded, she began:

'No, you are free to go, Almar. Shall I ask Clark to get your luggage together? Clark, would you please pack up Almar's things and get the motor home ready. It will be a fairly long trip, so you'd better stock the fridge.'

At the bar Clark closed the dishwasher which he had been stacking with dirty glasses and ashtrays, and went out. Rita looked at The Doctor as if to confirm that she had given the right answer, and he took over again:

'If you want to leave, Almar, we would be glad if you would cooperate with us by keeping the curtains in the motor home drawn. We want to make sure that our refuge, what did you call it, Ginnungagap, wasn't it? Yes, we want to make sure that it doesn't become common knowledge.'

Almar seemed uncertain, and for a while they were silent. Reflectively, the author drank the rest of the inky cocktail from his glass:

'And presumably the contract for *Bernhard Zero* is to be dropped? It was just bait to lure me out here and offer me this, this, well, I don't quite know how to interpret it.'

The Doctor studied Almar for a moment with a disappointed look:

'No, my friend, the book contract still stands, no matter what happens between us with this business that you don't seem to understand. I admit that book publishing is not our speciality. But we at the Small Firm are not small-minded. We

101

will get the book published through a good colleague of my acquaintance. The contract is a done deal, and not connected with the matter under discussion. Except if being published in the United States will propel you to ask if your attitude to life alters depending on whether you are enjoying success at the time. Do I want to be in the world in good times, but not in bad ones? If that is so, the creature who is drinking the ink from his pen without noticing it is best described as an old sourpuss. As such, you would obviously not be the right man for the friendly takeover.'

Almar looked searchingly at his glass before transferring his gaze to The Doctor:

'I think this is rather a silly discussion, if I may be so blunt as to say so.'

'Because we are talking about your basic existential feeling in connection with a potential of a business deal? Does it awaken a sense of shame in the innocent young man? Is the man who ought to be able to scrutinise everything offended? Or can we talk together like men here?'

Solomon looked Almar straight in the eye, and waited for a reaction. Almar shrugged and shook the ice cube in his glass as though he were ringing for invisible help. The Doctor continued boldly:

'Although it is in our business interests that you take part in the project, we are not pushing you to do anything. And I expect you can hear that although we are friendly, because the process is friendly, we are neither pampering you nor trying to pull the wool over your eyes and make you believe one thing or another. We rather dissuade you, as we are not making any profit from setting an extremely expensive and time-consuming takeover in motion and then ending up with one of the parties withdrawing in midstream. That kind of thing could result in mistrust, discontent and the end of our friendship. The only thing we are doing at this stage is to point out that the possibility of improving your life by disappearing is real. You have talked about it, you have written about it. If you haven't simply used the angst meter to check the quality and type of existence in order to appear thoughtful in the eyes of your colleagues, if you meant something with your books that says that deep inside you want to escape the yoke and burdens of existence, if you mean something by what you are in the eyes of thinking people, then this is the option we have to offer you. You are lucky because this is a path out of life that up to this point in history has been impassable, and today is available only to the chosen few. So, few, in fact, that I know personally all the people who have followed it.'

'Why me?'

'Here chance decides everything, as indeed everything that matters. Which says even more about how fortunate you are, Almar. But, so that we can be completely sure that the path is clear, it would be good if you would be so kind as to take some tests for us. It's easier for us to conduct them here, where the equipment is available.'

'I'm not going to take any damn tests, that's for sure.'

The silence at the table was oppressive until Clark arrived to say that the bags were ready. No one gave him the slightest attention. He went back into the bar and continued to stack the dishwasher. Almar Logi was thoughtful, Dr. Epstein exhausted, but Rita seemed excited. The Doctor looked at her, snapped his fingers at Clark and told him to put on some music and bring two Margaritas. Then he stood up.

'We don't need to solve the riddle of existence tonight, dear children. Almar, you are only now learning that there's a way out that is best for everyone. For your wife Hildur, and even for your son Bjartur, who knows?'

Rita frowned, as though Solomon had gone too far. Almar wore a fixed expression, as if he had been caught red-handed in some crime. Dr. Epstein yawned for a moment, his hand to his mouth.

'Forgive me, I'm tired, and have begun to ramble.'

Rita got up, put her hand on Almar's shoulder and rubbed it gently. The author gazed at her in a kind of trance.

'Increase the volume, Clark, and let them dance,' called The Doctor.' I'm going up to the house to sleep. Rita will explain things for you in more detail if there's anything you don't understand. Good night.'

Soon after The Doctor left, Clark placed two green cocktails on the counter and told them to serve themselves if they wanted any more. He, too, went to bed.

Starkaður watched Almar and Rita dancing cheek to cheek. Almar looked like a ghost, while Rita's eyes were dreamy. He could not ward off the thought that this was a waltz of death. Rita was whispering into the author's ear, but Starkaður could not make out the words. They seemed to have enough to talk about. The song came to an end, and Rita looked straight into the camera, staring from the screen with large eyes. For an instant Starkaður felt she was looking at him. Her expression was not nearly as kind as it had been when she looked at Almar Logi throughout the evening. She loosened her embrace but held her partner with one hand, and bent down under the bar counter. She seemed to be looking for something, until the screen went blank.

*

The following evening the motorhome set off with Almar Logi

104

aboard and Dr. Epstein invited Starkaður to dine with him on board the yacht. Rita was present, but Starkaður felt she was not herself. She was strangely abstracted, and far better-looking than he had thought her hitherto. He could not help thinking that something had happened between Almar Logi and her during the night. Then that was another sign that the author led a more fulfilling life than he did. Starkaður wondered why he had never provoked this mysterious expression on her face. An expression that without a doubt changed her into a beautiful woman.

After dinner, when Rita had gone to bed, he and The Doctor put on sailor sweaters and went out on deck where they sat on folding chairs with blankets on their laps, each holding a shotgun. On a glass table between them stood two glasses of sherry. The Doctor looked up at the reddening sky as he spoke:

'You must bear in mind, Starkaður, that we are entirely impartial in the matter of the friendly takeover. The Small Firm is only an intermediary. We are not with you rather than with Almar, or with Almar rather than with you. We stand with you both, equally and wholeheartedly. Almar is fixed in existence against his will. In him existence has created a hypersensitive consciousness that never asked for it and is caught in its own fluorescent spider's web. You, Starkaður, however, are full of longing for existence, but society has shut you out. The Small Firm is in the process of solving your double existential problem with a single action. In the end that will not only be to your benefit but also to everyone in your environment. I don't deny that we take a generous commission for it, as we are talking about the treatment of a basic problem of existence. No one else offers this today.

'But this is of little importance unless Almar Logi decides to come on board and work with us. Once again, our task is to wait. The quality you need most of all if the reputation operation is to succeed is patience, I expect you are starting to figure that out. Even if Almar decides to join us, you cannot breathe a sigh of relief and think that all is sealed. Only then will your stamina be put to the test, for more and more new circumstances will arise, in which a countless number of things may go wrong. But if the treatment fails at that stage, I am afraid I cannot reimburse you, as then the weight of responsibility lies on you rather than on me. But still, I will guide you to the end, and if you follow my advice there is a decent chance that you will both reach the destinations you desire. One out of a meaningless existence that he has none the less enriched with more meaning than most. The other into a good and meaningful life where people love him and take him seriously.'

The Doctor's voice became increasingly distant as two geese approached the yacht in rapid flight. When they were in range, he sprang to his feet, aimed and fired two shots. There was a sudden splash on the lake as one of the brids fell. The other veered off its trajectory, but still maintained its speed. Starkaður stood up and aimed. As he watched the wings propel the bird through the air like oars, he was fascinated by the soft screeching sound that accompanied the movement. With his finger, he stroked the trigger, but could not bring himself to press it.

13

On the territory of the Small Firm Starkaður could be himself, and so it was a setback for him to return to Iceland and need to adopt the dorkish disguise again. He told no one of his arrival, and felt how thoroughly empty his life in Reykjavik had become. Why was he struggling for acceptance again in this god-forsaken country?

Clark had let him have his phone back when they set off in the motor home, and he could finally browse his email on the Web. He had five messages from Janus Andersen, his lawyer in London. Janus outlined how matters stood, and the first four messages were formal ones. But in the fifth message he said he assumed that Starkaður had fallen on dark times, because he did not answer. He had now had a glass or two and would therefore allow himself to write not only as Starkaður's lawyer, but also as a friend who owed him a lot. He began by saying that the demands from the Icelandic state prosecutor meant there was no option other than looking reality in the face. If Starkaður was going to keep his business going from prison, that would be feasible, but he would have to prepare himself well if he was going to persevere with it. In a psychological sense eight years was life imprisonment, as that was the time it usually took to break a man down. However, there were exceptions, such as Albert Speer, who was Hitler's architect during the war and was sentenced to twenty years in Berlin's Spandau prison. Upon his release, he walked smartly out of the gates and wrote the book *Erinnerungen*, which in the lawyer's opinion was the best book on the Third Reich. Some argued that the fact the Germans were not defeated a year earlier was due to one man, Albert Speer. As an especially qualified interior minister, he had kept armament production going despite the constant bombing. In prison, he associated with no one except a few of the worst war criminals of the twentieth century who despised him as a traitor. In the darkness of his cell he wrote about them with stolen pens on toilet paper. Later, when published, these secret diaries revealed how he managed to survive twenty years in prison without losing heart. He had, for example, used the exercise periods to do gardening and walk up and down the yard. He measured the length of his walks and entered them on a map. In his imagination, he walked from Berlin to the land of the rising sun, and tried to obtain knowledge of the places he visited on his way by reading books. Starkaður would probably receive a sentence of eight to ten years, and would have to organise his time, like Speer. He could write a book about his career as a financial speculator, which would be sold abroad. That way he could keep his sanity in prison and even use his jail time as publicity for the book.

Starkaður sat at home in the rotating chair in front of his laptop with a bottle of brandy in his hand, trying to remember why he had chosen this wretched fate rather than the sweet life of Charles P. Harvey in India.

Rita did not arrive until half past eleven. She walked up the illuminated steps to the house in a green skirt and yellow, flat-soled shoes, looking tired and holding a pink knit sweater, one sleeve of which trailed on the paving. Starkaður fancied that there was lipstick left only at the corners of her mouth, the rest of it had been kissed away. She had been out a lot since they got back to Iceland, said she had to work on the reputation project. She meant that she had had to meet Almar Logi. For a week, she did not give away any more than that. Meanwhile Clark moved about the first floor as if it were his home and used the fitness studio in the basement at night. Sometimes Starkaður did weightlifting with him and tried to talk to him about other things besides the reputation project, without success. Clark used the days to create a workroom and laboratory for the project in a warehouse the Small Firm had rented in Grindavik. Almar Logi's participation was not assured, but since Rita and Clark were now working on Starkaður's payroll, Dr. Epstein had allocated tasks to all three of them to work on, until the project had reached a stage where he had a reason to come to Iceland himself. Rita was to focus on Almar Logi and open a way into the project for him. She made Starkaður read the author's books and all the information about him that was available online. He read reviews of his books which she photocopied at the National Library, practiced answering literary questions for interviews, studied his family tree and the people who were part of it. She put together a rough biographical overview of Almar she wanted him to learn by heart. She said it was a basic skeleton which would later be fleshed out with much more information, so detailed that it would beat all the biographies that Starkaður had ever read. From the overview, it emerged who Almar's parents were, where they had been living when he was born and all the places Almar had lived in to date. She had established what schools he had attended and some summers were being clarified in broad lines while others had a question mark beside them. She had managed to put times and dates on two high school girlfriends, but neither were referred to by their full names or were given descriptions beyond the fact that one had been a serious blonde and the other a red-haired Amazon. From the overview, it emerged that he had been interested in writing since at the age of fourteen he began to keep a diary when on a language course in Germany. Starkaður also received a list of the author's teachers at Reykjavik High School and what courses he had taken at the University of Iceland, and who had taught them. He acquainted himself with some of the textbooks that Almar had read after Clark was given the task of obtaining them. In addition, Rita brought photocopies of several of the author's diaries, which said to Starkaður that their relationship must have become close. When he asked Clark at the gym what he thought about the relationship between Rita and Almar he felt that the supervisor became unusually reticent, and it occurred to him that perhaps Rita and Clark did not sleep in separate beds at night. The next morning, when Clark had gone to Grindavik, Starkaður went into Clark's room. It appeared that he slept there alone, and it was the same in Rita's room. She had left a pair of black panties on her bathroom floor, and for a moment he had the idea of picking them up to smell them, but he checked himself. However, he stood staring at them for a long time until he looked up and gazed at himself in the mirror. At first he was embarrassed, but then he smiled. He tried to give himself a long, relaxed look as he did sometimes to see if he was in balance. For a minute he managed this, but then his gaze slipped for a while and he thought he was looking at a stranger who resembled someone he knew. He went upstairs, lay down on the bed and opened one of Almar Logi's diaries from the period after the crash in which he described a meeting of the Dream Club:

From the minutes of a former Dreamer

The Dream Club turned 17 today, and we celebrated with cakes and coffee. Guðni and I, the pioneers, retold the story and recalled a few memorable members' dreams. After the celebrations, when the cakes were finished and everyone had left except Guðni and me, he told me a story of his friend, one of the finest jazzmen in the country. In the summer of 2007 he and his colleagues received an invitation to play two numbers at the summer house of a nouveau riche billionaire. For the gig, they would be handsomely paid. They turned up in an old van and parked on a barren moor. All the parking spaces were occupied by shiny luxury cars.

The band members were trooping in with their instruments when a doorman came running up to them and showed them round to the back door. From there they were led into the kitchen where a servant gave them a sign when they had to play their numbers. On completing their kitchen concert they were sent away without having met anyone except the servant, the doorman and the chefs.

They did not know that while they were playing a bet was being made in the parlour of the summer residence on whether the guests could tell the difference between live music and music from CDs. Much more was at stake in the bet than the musicians were paid for the concert.

When Guðni had finished telling the story we began to speculate on its message in connection with the elitism that prevailed under the protection of the President before the crash. For the story combines the vulgarity of the billionaires and their desire to be civilised.

Guðni said that the people in the ballroom wanted to be cultivated enough to distinguish live music from music played from a CD. But the ability to hear what was authentic only seemed to be important among others in the elite, those who could afford to take part in the bet.

The musicians, who were authentic, received a generous fee for their performance, but were otherwise treated as second-class citizens.

I agreed with Guðni, and added that the behaviour of the billionaires was logical, given their assumptions, as people who believed in elitism could hardly see the purpose of chatting unnecessarily with a group outside the circle of the elite. What would they gain from it? Guðni thought the story expressed a divided position on culture, a position that was not tenable. The opinion was that the billionaire was above culture. He ought to be able to recognize what was alive and authentic when it came along, and use that skill to extort money from others in the elite. He should be able to bet on culture just as he bet on horse races and anything else he preferred.

He rounded this off by saying that when elitism and individualism went this far, all human sympathy disappeared and the childishness behind the attitude was revealed.

14

On the twelfth day of his return to Iceland, Starkaður had had enough of diaries and the silence in the house. In the evening, he sat down at the table in the vestibule with a bottle of Camus, having decided to lie in wait for Rita, no matter when she arrived. He had drunk a quarter of the bottle by the time she appeared, slightly unsteady on high heels, he thought. He stared at her searchingly:

'Were you putting on your lipstick?'

She laughed coldly. Starkaður knew that he had to accept this as an answer, and tried to soften his tone:

'By the way, how is it going with Almar Logi, is he on board the project?'

Rita kicked off her shoes and stormed in, not even responding with laughter this time. Starkaður followed her to the bar in the parlour. She was going to help herself to a drink but Starkaður dimly recalled that he was still master of the household, at least in the eyes of these foreigners whom he did not know, but who as far as he knew were on his payroll. He went into the bar and prepared two gin and tonics. When Rita held her glass, she stretched it towards him:

'Cheers!'

Starkaður kept his glass to himself, as she had said something ridiculous.

'For what, damn it? That I've thrown away millions on nonsense?'

They were silent, and turned to sipping the gin. Rita looked at the portrait of Starkaður that hung over the bar. It was very accurate in terms of the head and upper body, but got rougher towards the edges, where the colours were expressionistic and the canvas and stretcher began to be visible. At the top there was a rococo-style frame pattern on the unframed work, as if the artist were mocking solemn frames. In the portrait Starkaður was holding a hand mirror that might also be a cell phone. The face was accurate in the reflection, but elsewhere unclear. Rita had got through half a glass, and on several occasions, had torn her eyes away from the painting, but then looked at it again. At last it was as if she gave up, and she said in annoyance:

'On the whole I can't stand self-satisfied portraits of billionaires, but there is something that I don't understand about this picture. There's something familiar about the fireplace, the pose, and yet there is also something strange about it, something...'

She looked at Starkaður who sighed wearily and studied the painting with his hands clasped behind his neck.

'I think finding the right pose is more difficult than people suppose. Do you know what I mean?'

'No.'

They looked at the painting as though they were waiting for the figure to come to life and reveal the secret. Rita stood up, went over to the picture and touched it. When she sat down again she still seemed as preoccupied as before.

'What do you mean?'

Starkaður answered as if he had thought about the subject too often to enjoy discussing it.

'It often happens when people have spent their life on the go, have really exerted themselves, given a lot of themselves without thinking of rest. Then unexpectedly, on a sofa or a bed, or out on a sun-lounger, or anywhere, they fall into the right pose. The fulfilment of all they have taken upon themselves, all they have done, showers over them and changes them slowly and calmly from within into the person they longed to be, but did not quite know how to. So they are as comfortable as they possibly can be. Their body is absolutely in the right place, in the correct orientation to existence. Like a small, complex part that fits exactly into the clockwork of being, so that it runs smoothly, and the spirit attains freedom. This is the moment when the world opens its secret portals and invites one into it. This is what most people miss when they find the right pose. They misjudge the sense of well-being, move too quickly, and the magic moment is gone. Or they simply fall asleep, and miss the inspiration.'

Rita smiled at his words.

'But not you, Starkaður, you didn't miss it.'

Expressionless, he looked at the picture as though he would rather talk to it than to Rita.

'Oh my God, yes, I did. I always miss the right pose. I blow it, just like everything else. You know, I'm such a klutz that Iceland's in a historic crisis because of me and my old pals who are being imprisoned one by one.'

'What about the picture then?' asked Rita, and there was sincerity in her voice.

'Well, that's the thing. Look, as you can see from the signature, it was painted in the golden year of 2007.'

'And for a portrait of a self-satisfied moneybag it's an unusually good picture. I don't know why that is, perhaps he's slightly making fun of you with the art historical analogy. I mean the allusion to childhood as self-love. Whatever it is, I sometimes find myself looking for something in it, and yet it's so extremely ordinary. What is it with this picture, Starkaður? Is your bottomless piggy bank hidden behind it? How does it come to have such a strong presence?'

115

'Even though I don't have one myself, you mean?'

Rita did not reply, but the silence radiated acceptance and curiosity.

'This is my moment you're looking at, Rita. Do you realise? This is Starkaður as he could be at his best. This is the essence of the life of a man who became a historic part of the destiny of a whole nation. I had been wired up continuously for several years and everything was going well for me, after I picked up a tidy sum from Russia. I was now on the list of the thousand richest people in the world, and was immersed in the game. It so happened that one day I was reading some boring documents in the parlour here. I crumpled them up and threw them in the fire. Then I slumped down over there in the corner of the sofa with one foot on the table, in one hand a glass of brandy and in the other my phone, which brushed against my three-day beard with a pleasant scraping sound.'

'Was this the pose?'

'This was it, exactly. All at once I felt that this was the pose, and had the sense not to move. It wasn't easy. The feeling of well-being poured over me, and I wanted to stand up and scream with happiness. But crazy luck kept me relaxed on the sofa. The meaning of my life stood open before me, and yet I wasn't exactly drunk and hadn't sniffed anything for a few months. I was so lucky to have a cell phone next to my ear. Blindly I called my assistant who had clearly been asleep as he repeatedly asked who he was talking to. I whispered that I had found the pose.'

'Eh? What kind of pose? What is this, really?'

'This is me, I'm telling you: I found the pose.'

'Are you alone?'

'Shhh, shut up, this is amazing. Find the best portrait painter in Iceland, wake him up and tell him to come here straight away to paint my portrait.'

'Now? Starkaður, do you know what time it is? And do you realise how many weeks it takes to paint a good portrait? Why don't you talk to him tomorrow?'

'Don't ask questions, just do it, we must seize this moment. It doesn't matter how long it takes and how much it costs. I'll pay ten times what he's asking.'

Rita laughed.

'And that's how you caught the moment.'

Starkaður was thoughtful.

'That's how I got a painting of my moment. It was possibly the only sensible thing I did for myself at that time. There, in the pleasant combination of light and shadows on the canvas, one can see what I was. And yes, I can see the ironic comparison with Balthus. And yes, I realised it only when I had paid for the work and someone pointed it out to me. Laugh. Judge me if you will. I still think that the built-in irony does nothing except maybe please the art snobs when they spot it. After a few decades, the painting will have historical value in the nation's hall of infamy– which, let me tell you, will be the most popular museum in town. I shall never find that pose again in my life, as things stand. I have put myself in a position that is contrary to everything. From now on I am always the wrong man in the wrong place. Everything around me is followed by insults. Women like you can't ask about a painting of me except with a sarcastic smile at best. The interest never goes further than a wish to hear something amusing and tasteless, to confirm what a first-class idiot I am. No matter what pose I adopt, it's laughable. Everything I say is comical. Even my fate isn't something that anyone takes seriously.'

Starkaður suddenly perceived that his monologue had at some point touched Rita, but that his self-pity was driving

117

her away again. He thought for a moment and continued:

'But I know the right moment, I know the feeling that accompanies it, and I have to find it again. That's why I looked for you people at the Small Firm, that's why...'

He saw that she had quickly lost all interest in the picture. He switched to a gentler tone:

'How is it going with us, Rita?'

'He's not setting any conditions.'

'No conditions?'

'No, Starkaður, he's not setting any conditions. Really, what did you expect! A specially trained contract team?'

'Er, no, I thought perhaps you were talking about The Doctor. As you can hear, I've been slightly disoriented during these last few days. All this diary reading, and nothing else. To tell you the truth, I don't really know what we're doing.'

'Come on, Starkaður, you don't have to play dumb with me. Though perhaps it's easier for you to pretend not to understand what the process is all about.'

Starkaður was relieved. At last he felt he knew where he was with her. He shook off the pathetic look and tried to be himself. It did not go well. Without expression, he lowered his gaze, and drank some more.

'And Almar is with us?'

'Yes he is, damn it.'

Rita shook her head, raised her glass and they drank a toast.

He had expected to feel happy, but was as sad as she was, to judge by her expression.

*

They were sat out on the lawn, watching the pale face of the

118

moon, when Starkaður asked:

'How come he hasn't set any conditions? This is business, isn't it? Haven't you taught him anything about negotiation techniques?'

When she replied, she looked at him thoughtfully, as if to determine whether he was thinking of Almar, or the rules of business in general.

'If he had set conditions, we wouldn't have the right type of person and we'd be pessimistic about the future. That's also why he got such a long time to think it over. So he didn't go on the defensive, you see, and start to think about conditions. But in the end, he didn't set any conditions.'

Starkaður perplexed lowered his gaze and turned his empty glass upside down on the grass. Saw that he had caught a fly, its wings were soaked in wine. Rita went on:

'There are, however, certain conditions that are imposed automatically in a friendly takeover. Condition he would most probably set himself if he spent more time thinking about everyday things.'

'What are you referring to?'

'Almar Logi, who else?'

'No –the conditions, the automatic ones– what are they?'

'Guess.'

Starkaður looked at the moon until his expression was entirely blank, and then glanced at Rita, who bailed him out:

'He'd want you to be a better dad than he has been, and give Bjartur all the things he hasn't given him. He'd want you to enlarge his apartment, pay for the car that's putting an excessive burden on him. And he'd want you to protect his good name and love Hildur and make her happier than he ever could. He'd want you to be a good companion to his mother and all his friends, and generally be the man he could have been, and more.'

'Hang on a minute, am I paying for a new, free and honourable life?'

'And that is exactly what you are getting, Starkaður.'

'But what about all these lists?'

'Lists. They're the description of a full and free life. If you think freedom's associated with something like flight, go on a flying course. Get a private pilot's licence.'

She looked at him as if she were waiting for him to object, but he said nothing.

'A good reputation never appears from thin air, if that's what you think. A good reputation is based on solid connections with people. We begin on Tuesday morning. Dr. Epstein is coming on Monday.'

'Admirable.'

'What?'

'You remembered to use the pseudonym, even though you're a bit tipsy.'

'We're not all constantly tipsy. Are you listening to me, Starkaður?'

'Yep, with great attention.'

'We start at half past seven.'

'It's rather impersonal, isn't it? To meet first that way, I mean? Almar doesn't even know who I am. Or does he?

'This is business, Starkaður. Almar has agreed to it, and we shall just start the programme at once. You are to become acquainted slowly and formally. The spiritual business comes later, and then you can make friends. That's to say, if you choose to. For the present it's just ice-cold business, something you ought to be familiar with. And a lot of hard work. Harder than anything you've put your elbow to before, my dear chap.

Do you remember the rules?'

'Yes, I think so.'

'You think so?'

'You mean that we must never be seen together in public? That we must never mention each other's names in print or in everyday conversation? That I must have no contact with people from the past, neither mine nor his. And so on?'

Her look was now that of a weary mother talking to a stubborn child.

'It's important that you don't just remember these rules word for word, Starkaður, but follow them one hundred percent. Now the takeover is no longer an exciting idea but rather a heavy and sluggish reality. As ice-cold a business as business can be.'

15

Dr. Epstein disliked anything connected with the friendly takeover being put down on paper or sent by email, and so during the work in the warehouse he used a blackboard and chalk. Each Monday afternoon he sketched in the project timetable and assessed how things were going. The process began on June 1, 2010 and was to be completed by June 1 the following year. The starting date was the day when Almar had decided to take part, and their first formal meeting took place at the warehouse in Grindavik. Since then six weeks had passed, and so far, The Doctor's plan had held steady. Waving a stick of chalk, he went over the main points such as work with the motion simulator, personality synchronisation, connection of memory and emotions, handwriting and vocabulary adjustment, coordination of education, hypnosis to regulate the disclosure of expression under the influence of alcohol, and more.

Starkaður stared fixedly down at the floor with fatigue until he saw a newspaper he had thrown away earlier in the day. On the back page, there was an article which said that in the week that followed he was to attend the preliminary hearing of his case in the District Court, but it had not been possible to contact him, and so the case would probably proceed in his absence. Across the newspaper there were footprints that he reckoned were The Doctor's. He bent further over the paper to get a better view of the photograph of himself. Under the table he saw that Rita, who sat opposite him, had her hand on Almar's thigh.

He picked up the newspaper, wiped the sand off the

wanted mugshot the reporter appeared to have carefully chosen, and looked at The Doctor. Behind him was the project timetable. It said that the enlargement of Almar's apartment would be completed when Starkaður had recovered after plastic surgery, because then they would both be living there for a while. There was a rattle off when the surgery take place, when the assault on Almar would be staged, when they should start to exchange roles in public, and when Almar would go for the final operation.

The Doctor was talking about the happiness formula of Arne Næss, where the spark of life had a multiplying effect, but Starkaður did not take in his words. He was contemplating the apparatus. There was the voice recognition device which registered conversations immediately and showed graphically where the stresses were different. There was the screen of the motion simulator with the reputation merchants in the dance loop that Clark always kept running for his amusement. Starkaður watched the figures wiggle their hips to the tune *Staying Alive*, and waited for what they called the peacock dance. Their styles of movement had become very similar but with the solo dance Starkaður always managed to make the warning lights flash. Almar thought he ought to keep the solo dance, as some day he would be able to give his friends a pleasant surprise. There were histograms of personality tests and intelligence tests which showed that although they scored differently in some areas, on the whole they were perceived as equals. The main difference was that Starkaður was a more extrovert character who scored higher in scientific subjects, while Almar was at the other end of the scale. There was the physical comparison, Starkaður was 188 centimetres, two centimetres taller than Almar, so that he was used to wearing flat-soled shoes, while Almar nowadays always wore inserts.

Starkaður was in better shape physically, perhaps because he was two and a half years younger than Almar. There was the precise assessment of scars and birthmarks that would have to be cleared up on the first trip abroad, as soon as ears and nose were coordinated. Starkaður doubted that the operation would make his nose any prettier: he would doubtless have to get used to having a knob on it. Likewise, he was not particularly happy about losing the cleft chin he had hated when he was a teenager, but had then reconciled himself to, and now actually felt was his best distinguishing feature.

Although Starkaður achieved more results in sports, dancing and most physical activities, Almar scored higher in reading body language, which Starkaður found strange. Almar did not make much use of his body for expression, but was very good at reading people's states of mind from their body language. It had also come as a surprise to Starkaður that he was much better at drawing than Almar, but that Almar found it easier to understand pictures, especially their symbolic meaning. The Doctor was not greatly concerned about areas where Starkaður was better, but just encouraged him to always be aware of the need to rein himself in there, and urged him to concentrate on those areas where he lagged behind Almar.

The most difficult part was related to Almar's thought associations and unusual use of language, storytelling ability, and very odd ideas, often based on the reading of strange books of which Starkaður only had time to read extracts. Almar's reading list, which he had kept from an early age, was too long for the project. However, this side of Almar only came to light on special occasions when he was in a good mood with friends who were as eccentric as he was. The Doctor encouraged Starkaður to focus instead on the author's more everyday and dampen appearance, and stick with it. Starkaður had read Almar's dream diaries, which contained 1139 dreams, and he remembered their contents even better than the author, who usually wrote them down as soon as he woke up, thought about them immediately afterwards, but then seemed mostly to forget them. It was the same with the diaries, Starkaður found it much easier to recall their content than did Almar. This pleased The Doctor, who said that the diaries simplified their task, especially since, although Almar very often forgot what he wrote, the diaries were a unique picture of his mental world on which Starkaður could draw, and shape into an Almar of his own.

The author always scored very high in emotional intelligence, while Starkaður had to make do with a poor average. He goggled at the histogram, which repeatedly showed this, and wondered how it could be. He thought it could not be possible, considering what the takeover involved as whole, if he understood correctly. He was never quite sure that the final stage of the process was what he thought it was, because he did not understand what was going through the author's mind as he took part. Sometimes it struck him that Almar and all the people at the Small Firm were playing with him, but he did not make heavy weather of it. Then all that would happen would be that he got what was coming to him and ended up in prison, as everything indicated he would. However, then at least he would have tried to find another way. He still thought it unlikely to be a conspiracy, and this made Almar's role even more mysterious. Could it be that deep inside the author wanted this? And if the process went where it seemed to be going, did he himself really want that?

When five minutes had passed without Starkaður showing any reaction, Solomon said:

'Well, you're all thoroughly fed up with this. So, let us

turn to Rita's next videotape. Hello, Starkaður, do you hear me.'

'Of course.'

'Welcome back.'

'Thanks.'

'Have you learned the text?'

Starkaður nodded.

The drama section was the most moving one at times, but when it went well was also the most fun. Rita had filmed Almar with a hidden camera in league with Hildur, Bjartur and friends. They watched the tapes, learned the roles and acted the scenes on stage. Thus, Starkaður stepped into Almar's role, and they could all direct him. Almar usually played one of the friends, Hildur, or Bjartur, and could then in passing explain why they reacted as they did, in his view. Rita had told Starkaður in confidence that Solomon also saw this as a way for Almar to say goodbye gradually. By looking at life as playacting, and experimenting with the roles of different friends and relatives, he was moving away from reality even more, saw it all more clearly from the outside than he already did. They often worked on scenes in English, which they all understood, like the discussion after the reading in New York, the time at the bar with Hildur and Rita afterwards, and when Almar first met The Doctor aboard the *Alba Rosa*. But this evening they were working on a few minutes from Almar's meeting with his friend Guðni at Café Súfistinn.

Rita had managed to film them with the camera of her laptop at the next table. They sat surrounded by empty cups and plates, the meeting of the Dream Club earlier in the day had evidently been well attended. Guðni recounted a dream in a humorous tone, but every so often gave his friend a worried look:

'I really only dreamt about you, Almar, so you should get a metaphysical interpretation ready. It was all a bit freaky.'

'That's not my fault.'

'I don't know, anyway I hope I haven't gone crazy.'

'Well, I thought we'd confirmed that long ago.'

'It has now acquired new dimensions. You were arrested by two policewomen.'

'Sounds familiar. Are you sure you were dreaming? Weren't you just drunk, and reading an old newspaper?'

'This would never have been publishable in a newspaper. Unless the tabloids have gone into porn.'

'Go on.'

'They took you into a prison cell, undressed you, and guess what.'

'I deny everything. What sort of connections do you have at the police station that I don't know about?'

'If you only knew.'

'A man has no privacy anymore.'

'Can I finish this, or not?'

'All right, go on.'

'What do you think happened next?'

'I know what I hope happened next.'

'They chopped you into little pieces.'

'Typical that the ladies cracked down on me just when I thought things were looking up.'

'You had it coming to you.'

'Definitely.'

'I mean, they made mincemeat of you. You were unrecognizable after what they did to you. And then they took you by force. I mean, you know, I woke up in such a state that I felt sad about being divorced and not having the wife to hold on to anymore.'

'This just means that our association is too close, Guðni. I herewith propose that we wind up the Dream Club.'

'I couldn't agree with you more, old chap. But that's not the end of it. When the sex was over you stood up laughing, put on such a nice suit that it seemed to have its own opinion on economic affairs, and was as loud-mouthed as a nouveau-riche billionaire. Said you'd lost face in the crash, or something to that effect, and grinned. I don't remember exactly what you said except for the final sentence which you ended with a mournful look.'

'What did I say?'

'It's so incredibly easy to be killed if you're a good man.'

'Sounds right. Remember that it's my sentence. I shall view it as plagiarism if you use it in The Naked Suitor.'

'Don't worry. You'll be mentioned as the speaker. Anyway, what do to you think it means?'

'I don't know. But it's probably got something to do with my arrest during the protests outside Parliament. You remember I told you that when I pressed forward with the crowd into the ladies' arms I noticed that behind their glass helmets they wore lipstick. They had put it on before they donned their riot suits, and fixed pepper spray in their belts. You're probably worried that your love affairs might be as bad as mine.'

'And the cocky billionaire, what does he represent?'

'Something to do with financial matters. Perhaps just that you're determined to fix them even though the bank has written you an uninspired letter. The sentence shows that you feel your kindness has led you astray.'

'I'm damned if I know, Almar. You've always interpreted my dreams correctly so far. But I don't know, it's as if something is changing. Sometimes I've felt that my dreams were more about you than me, these last few nights.'

When they had translated the text, performed it and discussed a few things, Dr. Epstein asked what line of work Guðni was in and why Almar thought he had dreamed this. Almar replied that he was a doctor of philosophy and taught at the

129

University of Iceland. He had probably dreamed this because he unconsciously realised that major changes were taking place in his friend's life.

Solomon froze the video and studied the eccentric Dream Club members for a long time. He asked why Guðni had called his dream interpretation into doubt.

'Because it was a very poor lie, and he's no fool.'

'Just what I was afraid of.'

Solomon turned off the video recorder and pronounced:

'If Dr. Guðni is not to become a problem later we shall have to give him particular attention where the fake assault is concerned.'

16

Every café has an invisible backdoor for misfits that leads into the warmth of bourgeois society, a warmth that lasts for as long as one's cup is still steaming. Starkaður ordered a coffee and stepped into the aquarium-like everyday life of Café Súfistinn. The lights from the street outside gleamed in trembling raindrops on the window pane. Almar Logi sat in his habitual place, scribbling in his diary just as he had done some five months earlier when Starkaður first noticed him. Now the friendly takeover had been running for twelve weeks, and although Starkaður thought he knew everything about Almar Logi, it was becoming clear to him that he did not know him at all.

As Dr. Epstein, had ordered, they did not exchange greetings when others were present. Starkaður was sure that The Doctor had travelled to the United States over the weekend, and that Clark and Rita were on a car trip in the West Fjords, so he was not worried that they might be seen together. When Starkaður placed his cup on the next table and sat down on the sofa a short way from him, Almar Logi did not lift his pen from the diary. Although they were having a day off from the process, Starkaður could not help sitting with his legs crossed and leaning forward like Almar Logi. He imagined that he was writing in a diary in the diverse, volatile handwriting he had very carefully studied. But what was he to write? For sure, he could not write about his life as it was these days.

When Starkaður sat down, Almar Logi appeared to have frozen with his pen at a large full stop in the diary. Starkaður stirred his cappuccino and looked at him. Putting down his writing things, the author picked up his phone and cigarettes. With not a glance in Starkaður's direction, he walked out. The waitress vanished into the kitchen alcove behind the service counter to prepare a sandwich for a customer. Starkaður reached for the diary and browsed through it in search of his name, was eager to know what Almar thought of him. Of course, the author was not allowed to write about the friendly takeover, but Starkaður doubted that a man with an obsession for recording things could skip it. He thumbed through the pages until his gaze halted at the back of the book. Then he turned back to the beginning of the entry for the previous day:

August 20, 2010 Café Súfistinn

During the day, we worked mostly on vocabulary analysis and voice recognition. We went through the Icelandic and English alphabets to compare our pronunciations and identify the sounds where the differences are greatest. It was quite a tedious day, and we were glad to sit down, exhausted, at the round table, drink coffee and smoke. Rita sat hunched on the edge of her chair, and I could see the soft curve of her back, and her convex thighs. When she spoke, I felt there was extra meaning in everything that was addressed to me, and when she was silent it was because of something that came between us. The vibes from her had kept me going in the latter part of the day, and my body sought to keep up our strained and silent discussion, but I didn't know, any more than usual, how I ought to react to this. The machines were making the room warm, and she took off her sweater so that the peach-like shape of her breasts was visible under her T-shirt. I got it into my head that her breasts were giving off a fruity fragrance. This thought influenced my breathing, and I was bursting with claustrophobia. I longed to be left alone with the diary and forget the ridiculous situation we were in.

I had completely forgotten Starkaður. He often seems to be out of touch with himself and talking in accordance with standards of defence he created after some of his violent battles, which keep him going. His calculated behaviour often makes me lose concentration when he expresses himself, and I don't notice what he is saying. He has a way of fading into his surroundings while maintaining a strong, disconcerting presence. Like a wall that threatens to collapse on top of one in the next breath.

Suddenly The Doctor began to ply him with personal questions, something he hasn't done before. He wanted to know everything about Starkaður's love affairs, at once, without delay.

The blunt questions obviously took Starkaður by surprise. He fell silent, considering the matter. He looked as if he were trying to remember if he had ever had a life. Said in a hesitant voice, which was strangely like mine:

'Actually, I was once engaged to a woman who was being harassed by a stalker.'

He looked at The Doctor as if to assess whether this was the kind of thing he wanted to hear. The Doctor nodded encouragingly. Starkaður went on:

'For me the English word "stalker" was a mark of respect, and I always called him Mr. Stalker. Marta didn't think it was funny.'

Starkaður looked around him as if he could not believe anyone

133

would be interested to hear this. Solomon nodded irritably, indicating by gestures that he should continue.

'Marta's stalker sent her all sorts of messages and said he loved her passionately. Said he had never loved any other woman and never would. His love was unending and unconquerable. Again, and again he quoted the magazine Living Science in support of his feelings. Claimed that there it stood clearly in black and white that love was madness. He said that this mental illness was making him love her, and that was that. No matter what she said.

'Subsequently Marta became very insecure and began to ask me, over and over, if I loved her. The true answer that I gave her was simply: Yes, I loved her.

'But the answer was not enough. Next she asked:

'Why do you love me?

'I tried to lighten the tone a bit and said I had a mental illness that made me love her. She did not think it at all funny, and night after night she turned her back to me in bed. The situation was intolerable, and was made even worse by the constant sound of this urgent question in the apartment:

'Why do you love me?

'You know, if one is forced to think about it, this is a surprisingly difficult question. She might as well have demanded that I become psychic, and say what spirits our relationship had inherited from my family. Although I thought it was all rather hopeless, I did

134

the best I could. I began to list the reasons why I loved her, and thought at first that eventually I would convince her.

'I listed her physical characteristics, and the personal traits in her behaviour.

'In response she said that there were many petite women, dainty, dark-haired and good-humoured, who liked to have sex in the morning before they went to work.

'What if you meet another woman who meets the conditions of your love list even better than I do? Will you love her because she scores higher in your survey?

'Er, no! Of course, not.

'Then what do you mean by this endless list of features that thousands of women possess? Why do you love ME?'

I followed her round and round the apartment, listing more and more personal characteristics, but it was no use. In the end, she went off to sleep in another room.

Starkaður was absorbed in reading the diary when he saw Almar coming up the escalator from the bookstore below. He knew that he ought to put the book down, but could not. At first he was uncertain, but then felt he had a right to read about himself and his girlfriends, and frowned. Almar saw that he had the diary open in his lap, took the pack of Camels out of his trouser pocket, went to the escalator and disappeared down into the bookshop again. Starkaður watched Almar's retreating, feeling guilty about using up the man's free time. He decided to finish reading the entry quickly, and then clear off:

During the next few days I tried to give a complete and precise account of the reasons why I loved Marta, why we were a uniquely good match, since our characteristics fitted together like a living DNA complex. The clearer the arguments were, the more distant she became, until she called me a heartless bastard, and moved out in tears. I missed her, and to escape the constant thoughts about what I had done wrong, I immersed myself in work.

Some months later I made the acquaintance of the manageress of the café I visited every morning. Once, when paying, I told her that the service could not be better. She replied that the service could always be improved, to everyone's benefit. I looked surprised.

'Really? How good can it be?'

'If you only knew. What do you think?'

'Nothing, really. Except perhaps, well, if you were to bring the coffee to me at home.'

'Would that be better, perhaps?'

'Perhaps?'

'Yes.'

'No, it would be quite different. You're right. No matter how good the service is, it can always be a lot better.'

'There, you see.'

We parted with a smile. However, I did not hope for anything. On the Sunday morning, the weekend after I slept late, so I did not manage to drop by to pick up my coffee mug. I woke up to the sound of the doorbell. Hung over after the Saturday night, I opened the door. Ása stood there on the steps, compact and brunette, holding a mug of coffee, looking at me with feigned indignation. On the T-shirt above her breasts was a smiley badge. On top, it said: Better service.

'Wow, you do look a sight,' she said. 'Here, get this down you and tell me when you're finished. Meanwhile I won't look.'

Laughing, I invited her in, and gradually she brought more than a mug of coffee over the threshold.

A few months later she asked me over coffee one morning before we went our separate ways:

'Why do you love me?'

No stalker. No problems that I had noticed. Nothing.

Just the end-of-the-world question over the homely aroma of toast, marmalade and morning coffee.

I knew where the question was leading, came to a grinding halt and didn't answer. Just kissed her goodbye, which I said was love in action. Promised to answer when I got home.

At work, I began to think that I could not lose another girlfriend *because of this ridiculous frequently asked question. People might think I was incapable of staying in a relationship. I put off the morning meeting. Sat swilling coffee in the office, where I could write my concerns in the mist on the window: I DON'T KNOW HOW TO LOVE! With caffeine jitters and a pack of cigarettes I sneaked away from the secretary and went up to the roof to consider the matter. One thing I knew: I was not going to run around the apartment after a woman, desperately screeching that I loved her. I will never do that again. Emotion is a marketable product, but for anyone to want to buy it, it must be well packaged. So, I invited her for a ride in my car up to the summer cottage at Hellnar, where I made her a romantic three-course meal. In the hot tub under the cold eyes of the stars with the murmur of the ocean in the distance, I had planned to tell her why I loved her, but as she was silent I hoped that she had forgotten the question. Then it came clearly:*

'Well, then.'

'Well, then what?'

'Come on, you promised.'

There was no getting around it, and I blurted out:

'Look, Ása, you have many good qualities. But that is true of many women. When many women have the same positive qualities and there's always one who excels above all the rest, then in spite of her individualism, one can't always find the reasons in that person that proves conclusively why that one is the one to be loved. The person I love is one of thousands who possess the qualities that impress me. So why am I with her,

rather than one of the others? And why should I continue to be with her when there is always someone who excels her in what I love in her behaviour?'

'The answer lies, I think, in situations and atmosphere.

'In a certain place, at a certain time we were in situations where we were ready for each other, where we opened to each other like pearl shells on the seabed, and hit it off together. One situation after another came along in which the qualities that charmed us in each other's behaviour stopped being merely words, became a reality which we filled with our spirits and our lives. That way the situations brought us together. And what are situations? They are something we know almost nothing about. They are something that we end up in.

'So, I love you, Ása, because you are you, and we are meant to be together.'

That was all I said to her. By the end of the speech I made it perfectly clear with gestures that I wasn't open to further inquiries. The answer to the question had arrived, period. And sure, enough, she was satisfied with it. To prove it, she floated over to me and kissed me as her bikini drifted away. Said she found my answer intolerably cocksure. It reminded her of why she had fallen for me. She never asked again why I loved her. A year later, when she dismissed me, she said it was because I was too much on the move, and on the rare occasions when I was there, too distant. She wanted someone she could lean on, in whose arms she could sleep, with whom she could wake up early and start a family. Not someone who jumped out of bed immediately after sex to go to work. She said she loved me, but it would never work out, because I loved my job more than people.

I promised to be at home for at least nine months a year, but it was too late. We parted with the words that we loved each other. I remember that, as I closed the door and went to the bar, I felt that the whole thing was somehow tragicomic.

*

While telling the story Starkaður had not turned a hair. The narrative did not seem to affect him particularly, nor did he appear to find it remarkable in any way.

We sat at the table in silence until Solomon asked:

'Wait a minute, are you still fond of her?'

Starkaður glanced at us for the first time since he began talking, with a look of amazement. It was as if he had forgotten us.

'Er, no, not really. I've never given it any thought. Until now. Because you're asking about all this.'

I think what he says is true. He is one of those people whose life is elsewhere. Others can think about it and certainly feel it. He doesn't realise that his own love story is just as important as anyone else's, and that his reflections on it are as human and helpless as the thoughts of a lover more famous.

Rita stroked her hair and moved restlessly in her chair. She gave Starkaður a challenging look, which he did not notice. Finally, she could no longer restrain herself:

140

'Have you had no contact with her since she walked out after telling you she loved you?'

Starkaður looked at her as if he had ended the meeting but people were still to discussing the matter.

'No!'

His tired eyes surveyed us irritably until he sighed:

'Or rather, yes, once. Just once. But that was...'.

He fell silent, as if he had been talking too much. We all looked at him, as if for the first time. He tried his technique of sitting so still that he disappeared. But it was too late. Our curiosity was aroused.

'Oh, it was really nothing special.'

'What happened,' asked The Doctor. 'Did you pay her a visit?'

'I don't know whether you could call it a visit. Although I often thought about her when I was in India, I lost all contact with her. As I did with old friends in general, actually. So, a few days after I got out of prison and was about to begin a new life, I called on my grandmother. Ása and I had once given her a picture of us. I wanted to have a look at it.

'Ása and grandma always got along well together. In a way that I didn't understand. Grandma kept the picture in a chest of drawers in the room with photos of other members of the family.

I became absorbed in looking at it and gave a start when she said that they kept in touch on the Internet. She said that Ása was pregnant. She had met some waiter, whom she married. They built a villa in Kórahverfi.

'And you went to visit her even though she was living with someone?' Rita asked, shocked.

Starkaður gave her a vacant look:

'Grandma said she had seen their house put up for auction, and they were losing everything they owned. They were thinking of moving abroad and leaving their loans unpaid. Forgetting about it all and just declaring themselves bankrupt. At first Ása had considered having an abortion and struggling on here in Iceland. She didn't believe they could afford to run a family as things were. They were thinking of moving to Denmark. Her husband was there, looking for work and getting the lie of the land, so I decided to go and knock on her door.'

'Wasn't she surprised to see you?'

As soon as I got involved in the discussion of this important question, I realised that despite all the work in the warehouse, this was the first time I had spoken to Starkaður directly and sincerely. He seemed to find it perfectly natural that I should ask him about personal matters, and suddenly became more relaxed than I've ever seen him. For a long time, he said nothing, looking warmly at me. I perceived with surprise that I was probably the only person at the table to whom he was not, deep down, utterly indifferent.

'No, Almar Logi, she was just happy. She didn't accuse me of anything, as I had expected her to. After the treatment, I've received here in Iceland I found it particularly pleasant, I can tell you. All around her there were full boxes and suitcases. She said she was packing, and intended never to return. She clearly didn't want to talk about financial matters. I asked about them but she changed the subject and wanted to know what I had been up to. I didn't really have much to tell her. So, well, I just said goodbye to her with an awkward shake of the hand, and she wished me luck.

He was silent, and gave a sign that the story was over.

Rita shook her head and laughed, was about to say something, but Solomon cut her short with a wave of his hand. Clark went round with the coffee pot, filling our cups. The Doctor offered Starkaður a cigarette, lit it for him and gazed steadily at him. When Starkaður had blown out a few puffs of smoke, he looked at us one by one:

'All right. The next day I paid her debt. Just like that. I took pains to make it pass unnoticed, and thought there would be no consequences.

'But after a few weeks the tabloid press began to write about the story and as a result it all went haywire. Ása was called out as my concubine and it was stated that she had got pregnant without her husband knowing anything about it. It was said that he was going to divorce her. Litigation had begun because of the payments for the house. Some pension fund inspector I had never heard of thought he could trace the money in such a way that his fund would be entitled to it.

'I don't know what happened after that. I haven't asked Grandma for news of Ása. I would honestly rather not hear any more about it.

'All this taught me was that it was best to have no contact with anyone. Neither old girlfriends nor friends. Those people belonged to a life that was over. That was how it was. After that I began to think of ways of escaping from a completely worthless past. My reality is right here in the warehouse with you. As pathetic as it sounds.'

He looked at Solomon accusingly, as if to say: 'Are you satisfied now, isn't this what you wanted to hear?'

The atmosphere was awkward until The Doctor began to drone on about something concerning the day's work, the nature of the friendly takeover, and so on. No one listened to him. But it was good that he took it upon himself to smooth over the uncomfortable atmosphere. I remember that I sat and nodded, and said 'aha' from time to time, without hearing a word of what he was saying. I went over the story again in my mind to get it right, here in the diary. And now it is there – period.

My Americano is cold. This is undrinkable dishwater, and now it's past time for coffee. I had better get up and ask for fruit tea.

Starkaður put the diary down, closed his eyes, and rubbed them. Heard the waitress walking between the tables, clearing up. The clatter of cups came closer, but then all was quiet, except for the old familiar Chet Baker CD. He had forgotten the diary entry and sensed it now like a dream. He wished that when he opened his eyes he would see a smiling Ása in the chair opposite him, on her left breast a picture of a steaming, heart-shaped cup of coffee. On the black T-shirt, the red letters said: Enjoy! All that had happened since they split up had been nothing more than some strange psychological thriller they had rented from Video Central, hadn't understood much of and fallen asleep over. She would put her hands on his thighs, lean towards him and kiss him.

At the touch of the hot lips he gave a start, got up and walked out.

Almar Logi was leaning against the window of the bookstore, talking to someone who was making him laugh. On the paving slabs lay cigarette-ends and so many matches that they made Starkaður think of a fallen citadel. He remembered that outdoors Almar always used three matches to light up. His interlocutor, a tousle-haired fellow with a Fjællreven backpack on his shoulders, his neck bright red, seemed to have arrived from a long hike. While he spoke to Almar he wore his sunglasses back to front, so that it looked as though he had eyes in the back of his head. When he looked around and saw Starkaður, he turned out to be Dr. Guðni, the Dream Club member.

Instinctively Starkaður set off towards Tjörnin pond, as if he were going to Thingholt. After a few steps, he remembered that they had finished disinfecting the house the day before, and locked the place up: now he did not even have a door key to his home anymore. Dr. Epstein had said that now that the house was locked up and the plastic surgery lay ahead, for the next six or seven months he would meet no one but the reputation seller and the Small Firm's employees. He could say goodbye to some people first if he cared to, but no one was to suspect what the nature of the visit was.

Was there anyone to whom he had not yet mentally said goodbye? He thought about it.

Only one person came to mind.

17

As soon as Starkaður moved out, his old room had been turned into a combination of guest room and store cupboard. When he dropped in to see his grandmother for coffee a month later there were no visible signs that he had lived there for six years. He had gone to ask her to lend him some money for a few days to cover the rent insurance. She had very firmly refused; was not going to let him get used to borrowing money from people. It would be best if he learned to manage his own finances as soon as possible. He submitted to the lecture in silence, gazing at the bookshelves that covered the walls, the old furnishings that looked remarkably intact, considering they had been excavated after her childhood home was destroyed in an avalanche. It felt as it had done when he moved there at the age of fourteen: he found the apartment more like a museum than a home. He had gone about dejectedly, as if he might be asked right there and then to show an entry ticket he did not possess. Grandma, who had never said a word to him in anger, or ever encouraged him in anything, either, was a personification of the past. The tea that she constantly sipped was like a magic potion that made her immune to the flow of time.

Now, as he sat at her kitchen table, he remembered that when he was alone at home he had gone round and round the apartment, through the kitchen, into the dining room, into the parlour, through the TV room and back into the kitchen again. He had felt excited when he turned a corner in this environment that was at once reassuring and constantly strange. Felt as though suddenly someone smartly dressed might be standing there with a golden envelope that contained what he ought to do with his life. Sometimes in a subdued voice he said 'hello', as if to vigilant eyes he felt were watching him. But no one was watching him. There was no parent calling, there were no cousins wondering how his studies were going. He later realised that since he had drifted away from his parents at an early age, many people unconsciously viewed him as a troublesome brat, and hoped at best that he would avoid ending up as a reprobate like them. He now understood that the feeling that someone was watching him was the basic sense everyone has that life expects something of them, that fate awaits them full of expectation. Something that most often was absurd.

But perhaps in spite of it all the Three Fates are sitting in elegant chairs in this museum-like apartment, he thought now, holding an old cup that had been his late grandfather's. At any rate, I'm caught in the fateful spider's web of the nation that is dragging me down into the abyss, and will drown me if I don't manoeuvre nimbly.

Having received this awakening, Starkaður quickly got up, took *The Handcuffed King*, a biography of Harry Houdini, from the bookshelf and opened it at an illustration where Houdini had been submerged at sea, locked inside a safe. The thought that he knew exactly how the artist felt on the ocean bed made him smile.

Grandma had never been in the habit of listening to him. Instead, she remained silent and distant, and knitted, or delivered long monologues. She often told unremarkable stories, for example, about gloves that had been lost and then found again ten years later, stories that could take up to half an hour to tell and were tiring but also enlightening because of their detailed digressions about people and topics. Her memory was infallible, but as tedious to browse in as an old encyclopaedia, so Starkaður was always wary of asking her about the past. Now, when he had come to see the picture that he and Ása had given her when they were together, he wondered whether his grandma was the reason that he had never been interested in history.

The bourgeois stiffness of her childhood home accompanied her, and while he lived in her apartment formality surrounded everything like sea spray icing on an old pleasure steamer. With age, however, she became more cheerful, nowadays wore a constant smile and showed affection by touching. Starkaður scarcely recognised this cheerful, stooping woman who seemed to be celebrating her approach to the earth. In the parlour, she usually had the television on in the background, the radio at full blast in the kitchen and the newspapers open, scattered around the apartment, as she followed everything that happened in the world.

'I thought I'd be seeing you about now, Starky. You've come to attend your trial, haven't you?'

'Actually, I don't really know. I let the lawyers deal with those matters. I'm only here for two days. Just arrived, you see.'

'They say you bet aggressively against the króna, concealed a gigantic sum and I don't know what else. I can't make anything of it. Isn't it all a misunderstanding? One lawyer said you'll get at least nine years. That's quite a long time.'

'Longer than I lived here with you, grandma. You keep an eye on everything, as usual. May I turn the radio down a little, please?'

Starkaður did not wait for an answer, reached towards the radio set, but grandma stopped him before he could turn down the volume, and exclaimed:

'Reporters keep calling and asking where you are and what you're doing!'

'I've been in India a lot!'

'Pah. They have me saying all kinds of things that I never said.'

'Just remember, if they get in touch again, you haven't heard from me for months.'

Starkaður was not sure she had taken this in, and repeated it directly into her hearing aid. She nodded, and continued her oratory:

'Don't believe what you read in the newspapers about what I'm supposed to have said. They've turned my words inside out so often and distorted them with rationalizations so much that I don't know what they're writing any more. I only remember what I said, and it was nothing but good things about you. For you were always very quiet, Starkaður. I never used to notice you about the place, more often than not.'

Grandma made one slice of toast after another for him while she gave a speech, with many pedantically detailed digressions, about her dealings with the press in connection with his case. Starkaður was unable to stay focused, but whenever there was a pause he always asked about the same thing. The photo of Ása and him.

He knew that if he were to talk about himself he would have to lie, which could soon arouse suspicion, so he merely looked at her to fix her in his memory. In between, he browsed through the family album. He stopped at a black-and-white photo of his parents, happy on the dance floor before they divorced and met other dancing partners whom they also abandoned. One thing certain was that he had no need to say goodbye to his parents. He had done that even before he became a teenager.

It looked as though the visit would end as it always did, he reading and she talking about something he could no longer hear. When he stood at the front door she suddenly put her arms round him and embraced him. A minute went by. His back was getting tired and he wanted to straighten up, but she did not let go. Suddenly he felt tears well up in the corners of his eyes. He had a mental picture of himself giving her money, and then he knew how he felt. But the cash would probably find its way straight to his father, so he dismissed the idea. He took a few deep breaths, and when she finally released him she seemed to notice nothing out of the ordinary in his expression. She took off his coat and drew him back with her into the kitchen.

'You're not in any hurry. Who knows when we'll see each other again. I've reserved a space in Fossvogur Cemetery next to your grandfather, and the door you could vanish through may very well have heavy locks on the outside. Now sit down and tell me something about yourself. You seem a bit different. I can hardly recognise you. Was it India that made you like this? What was it like?'

It took Starkaður a moment or two to realise that total silence reigned in the apartment. He could hardly remember a time when she had not had both television and radio on. And now she wanted him to talk. He looked at her thoughtfully and it occurred to him that he had never talked openly to his grandmother. This was the last chance. Perhaps this was his last opportunity to talk openly to anyone at all. He contemplated the back of her hand with its prominent veins and could count the bones in it. All the flesh seemed to have gone to the grave before her, and it would probably not be long before she followed. For six years, she had supported him. He had never thanked her. He felt that he owed her, even if only for one genuine moment, put his hand quickly on the back of hers and said the first thing that came into his mind:

151

'You know, Grandma, it costs next to nothing to stay at a five-star hotel in India and rent a car, a driver and a guide who are available when one rings for them. Yes, I mean it. One doesn't have to worry about a thing. If one trashes the room one night, all one needs to do is to go for a long breakfast and a swim the next day. On one's return, everything is clean and comfortable. Just so. One's clothes folded, ironed, even fresh from the dry cleaner. The desk tidied up, new towels in the bathroom, a basket of fresh fruit, bottles of wine as a gift from the hotel. One can appear to be on top of things even though one hasn't a sensible cell in one's brain and all one can do is wander about with one's glass between hotel suite parties.

'Then, when one grows tired of people and the sweet life one can always go for a massage and relax. I can tell you, grandma, that I developed the weirdest routine I have ever had in my life when I stayed at the Imperial Hotel in New Delhi. I watched TV until morning, slept until noon, then went for a swim and had lunch at the Royal Lounge, where I had a reserved table in a corner by the aquarium. I turned my back on the main restaurant, as I couldn't stand other people any more. Yet I missed human contact a bit, so I went for a massage. It's safe to say that there I lost myself, as so often in life. For the first time in many months I relaxed. I lay down on the bench and stared at a floating lotus flower in a bowl, and as soon as the masseur began to lubricate my shoulders with hot oils and drill his fingers into my stiff back I slipped into another world and fell asleep. Woke up only to turn over. I was so pleased with the long-desired rest that I ordered more and more massage sessions each day until I began to spend the whole of the afternoon that way. I have no doubt that I'm the most massaged man in Icelandic history.

'I could have ended my days being massaged to death,

Grandma. But after two months I snapped out of it when I got an invitation from the Icelandic ambassador to attend a garden party in honour of our President's visit to India. The invitation surprised me. I hadn't told anyone at home of my travels in India. In the past, I always began by letting my assistants inform the Icelandic embassy that I was on the move and was thus automatically attending the cocktail parties that ruled the world. The feeling there was that we were the elite of life who governed the future by exchanging humorous stories, the future came to the masses through our laughter that chinked like gold coins falling into a treasure chest. Yes, this was the golden cream of the world's crop, whose cocktail glasses chimed rhythmically in a modernistic accompaniment to their laughter and toasts. But I was sure that this time the entertaining numbers would be at my expense, and the future would come to the world through the laughter of someone other than I.

'Because people in town knew about me, I decided to say goodbye to the masseur, whom by then I saw as my friend, we still corresponded, and went straight off to Jaipur that night. After living in the air-conditioned hotel for over two months, it was a real change to step out into the saturated air pollution. My driver had had little to do but polish my car for eight weeks, and was glad to see me. He suggested that we shouldn't go out on the motorway immediately because of the trucks that were on the move in the evening, but I didn't listen to him. I am glad I didn't, for the experience of the Indian motorway is the best experience of the struggle of life itself.

'The Indian motorway is like a long running jump taken by a man trying to soar up from the dirt of the earth. The endless road is just endless poverty. People sleep under whatever garbage they find at the side of the road and on traffic islands, entire families live in huts that are separated from the motorway by nothing but dust and pollution. I saw a ragged boy fighting a laughing monkey that was stealing food from him, and sacred cows living the good life eating newspapers that no one has read, but many used as sheets and blankets. The sight that pleased me most was that of a cow eating the Indian *Financial Times* with great relish. I thought it said everything about this magnificent land. On car roofs and the backs of trucks flashed the brightly coloured veils of sleeping children who had left the cardboard boxes in which they grew up to discover where the wheel of fortune would throw them out. On the road one could see that poverty is the law of the world, it is the rule and always will be. But why did I never see undernourished people? I wondered a lot about that. Once when the car got stuck in a nightmarish traffic jam I received an answer to the question. I saw a destitute man trying to support himself by selling tea in plastic cups. His stall was an upturned wooden crate he had patched together from scrap timber. As he stood behind the crate his expression changed, and he became very grave. When a vagrant came past, he stepped out in the man's way, handing him a dry wheat cake and a cup of steaming tea, without a word. The vagrant accepted the meal in majestic silence, squatted down and munched it with the stick between his legs. His eyes, bloodshot and staring, had seen everything. The stall-owner watched him proudly. As though he were the richest man in the world because he could offer him a free meal.

'This incident showed me the earth's most advanced culture, and it begins in the most extreme poverty. All attempts to take poverty away from humanity end in a tragic perversion of nature. The soul springs from poverty beautiful and intact, but is disfigured by wealth. The impoverished soul is the visible image of holiness in the world. Do you hear that, Grandma? Indians know this better than anyone, as for them there is nothing more natural than that a tiny number of nobles should have all the gauze and finery, while everyone else treads in a circle around them as if they were gods, massaging them with warm scented oils from morning to night. There are eight hundred million poor people in India. You hear that, Grandma? Eight hundred million! That's twice the entire population of Europe. Does it make any sense to work out how much money each person has when the situation in the world is like that? One could just as well speculate on the distribution of ownership when gazing at the stars! If anyone planned to change this, they'd need to revise the laws of nature and realign the orbits of the planets while they were about it.

'On the Jaipur trip I made an economic experiment. I changed ten thousand rupees into thousand rupee notes at the bank and went down to the old royal palace in downtown Jaipur, where I stood outside and handed them out, one at a time. I can tell you that everyone went crazy. I nearly choked with laughter as I was trampled underfoot by eager paupers. I'm ashamed to tell you, Grandma, because I did it for scientific purposes, that I don't remember any more of what happened. Except that I regained consciousness under a fruit stall in the marketplace with police wielding night sticks over me. Perhaps the experiment failed because I came to before I had proved the theory. The most natural outcome would have been for me to be crushed by the world's most highly-strung goddess, poverty. That would have confirmed the hypothesis that the rich should not try to please the poor. Perhaps it was my driver who obstructed the progress of science. The first thing I saw was him talking to the police, and then setting them on children and elders with clubs.

'I staggered to my feet, took a cab to the airport and could not help laughing all the way. It was painful laughter, because my whole body was crippled after a night of violent love with the goddess of poverty.

'At the airport I went for a massage and sauna and bought a ticket on British Airways, I don't recall where to. I just wanted to fly with them, because of the service. Their business class is excellent: fully flat bed, nice curtains to draw, wonderful selection of wines. Outside the window an endless expanse and the hum of the engines like a beautiful lullaby sung by a choir of angels. Then it's pleasant to take off one's sleep mask in the middle of a dream and look outside. The waves below are like royal blue Chinese silk in a jewellery casket, the moon like a diamond on a silver ring. The casket will soon be closed and given to the day as a morning gift.

'The day on board always just as splendid. The atmosphere of roaming between books, newspapers, films, CDs and desultory pseudo-conversations with flight attendants and other rootless creatures with false smiles. A living, fragmentary atmosphere. The everyday stimulus twittering like a symphony orchestra in one's half-dreaming head, endlessly tuning up but never managing to play because the conductor never appears on the platform. Eventually the aircraft sinks like a penis that has left white stains of semen all over the sky. Turn off your cell phones! Seats in the upright position! Everyone in straight rows of mortality! People gape at the earth's greedily approaching maw, dull gazes meet, people begin to gather their things, pondering what may be coming next. The plane's testicles hammer the runway with a painful wail as it sinks into earthly existence, full of stupid banality. What country is this? What time is it? What's the weather like? Where is a hand that I can lead into the walkway, through the terminal, onto the next plane?

'On the next flight I ordered two seats by mistake, and in my mind Ása sat beside me. I fell asleep, and when I woke up remembered what she had once said to me on a flight.

'Hey, you just dropped off.'

'I began to wonder at the strangeness of this choice of words seven kilometres above the earth.'

'You dropped off, Starkaður.'

He looked up at his grandmother.

'Grandma, I wanted to ask if I could have the photo of Ása and me sailing.'

18

At the heavy wheel of the old Volvo on the way south to the warehouse he tried to focus, but the mind wandered in all directions. In accordance with the medical advice he had received for the forthcoming procedures he had neither smoked nor touched alcohol for ten days. In the midst of the chaos his mind was hammeringly clear.

The warehouse was now to be his home for at least the next six months, while the wounds healed. Almar Logi and the trio from the Small Firm would come and work on the process during the daytime, and then he would be alone there every night. The first plastic surgery procedure would take place in Dortmund the following day. Once it had been carried out there was no turning back. The suitcases stood ready in the lobby along with holdalls containing forged identity documents, but the Epsteins, Clark and Solomon, who were to accompany him, had not arrived. Starkaður paced the floor of the warehouse and talked to himself out loud:

'If I pull out now, no harm will be done. I will just pay the Firm compensation on top of all that I've already paid, but will escape the final sum. I could even let Almar have something for the time he has put into this. Also, he's already received quite a lot for his trouble. The expansion of the apartment is well advanced, and *Bernhard Zero* has been published in the United States. Admittedly in a small print run, but it's a good quality edition and for a prestigious book club. It's only absurd that at some point it will be considered a book by me. And what ought I to write when I become an author? I don't even know what to write in the diaries that would be an honest account. I could hardly write about the takeover in the form of a novel. Wouldn't that be rather brazen? How would I write about myself, or Almar Logi, rather? Perhaps I could write interviews with my relatives, or rather, Starkaður's, like Grandma, and thereby have an influence on the memory of ... what? Me or him?'

As he wandered around the warehouse he peeked into every nook and cranny, and was met by gloomy reflection in screens and windowpanes. He considered the fact that this man had been disguised and in hiding for so long that he was almost a stranger to himself. And yet. This was the image that had always followed him like a loyal friend. Would he really have to destroy his cleft chin so his countrymen viewed him as a normal person? Was there no other way? He clutched his head and forced himself to stand still and think. Nothing came to mind. He forgot himself in a rhythmic humming until in his mind's eye he saw himself take off his clothes and lie down on a soft bed. As he lay there and relaxed, he suddenly saw himself lying naked, dead on the floor. He had inadvertently undressed from his own body. But then who lay here, under the quilt? He started up from his daydream and shook his head:

'No, it's better to walk.'

He strode off across the warehouse floor again, and began to call out:

'Hello, is there anyone here with a gilded envelope for me? You there in the corner, tell me, what's expected of me? Am I to drown in a safe on the seabed like Houdini? Because the little door got bent and can't be opened? Would that be better? Hello! I just want to talk to ordinary people about ordinary things. Hello! What do you think of the weather?'

In a different voice, he answered himself:

159

'The weather is changeable today!'

He giggled and felt better in the old trance-like gait into which he had so often fallen when he was home alone at Grandma's as a teenager. As he marched with heavy steps he was seized by a tingling expectation. As if life were about to pull something out of the magic hat that belonged to the goddess of destiny, something just for him. Thought to himself that despite everything he was doing something he had never imagined he would do in his life. Was that not in itself exciting? The thoughts that had descended on him wilted when the trance-like atmosphere took over.

'Hello, I'm here, open to the Fates, hello, hello, hell –'

'HELLO, we hear you, Starkaður, are you coming!?'

The imperious answer brought him up short. Dr. Epstein had sneaked quietly into the porch and stood there ready in all his brilliant white haired-ness, laughing along with Clark. Starkaður had quite forgotten that he was wearing a microphone. They had been able to eavesdrop on everything that had taken place both at his Grandmother's and in the warehouse, though they had not understood much of it. When The Doctor stopped laughing he reached into Starkaður's jacket to remove the microphone. Asked:

'Well, are you ready to metamorphose? Or did you have some hesitations after you said goodbye? I heard you saying an awful lot to your Grandma. I didn't know you could talk so much.'

Starkaður noticed that he had the photo of Ása in his hand, and that he had already managed to crumple it. He smoothed it out and put it carefully in his wallet. He wanted to say something to The Doctor, but could not think of anything, and looked at him in silence. Thought fleetingly that in this body the lifespan of his soul was at an end. He would start thinking again when the face in the mirror was to the liking of the outside world. And then he would be able to think of something other than what he had lost, would even be able to dream about the future. Solomon took his holdall and put his hand on his shoulder to lead him out:

'At least you had someone to say goodbye to, Starkaður. My last two customers had no one. The buyer before them had six people he wanted a whole month to say goodbye to. We had to face the fact that we had a bad apple on our hands.'

Starkaður had heard The Doctor talk about the bad apple every now and then. It was the only takeover of the six the Small Firm had organised that had gone wrong. He thought he saw a look of revulsion appear on Clark's face at the mention of the bad apple, but thought it best not to ask.

Clark picked up his suitcase and held the front door open. Although he gave a friendly grin when Starkaður passed him, his eyes were as devoid of radiance as ever.

19

Starkaður had gone under the knife six times, and after comparing him and Almar, the Doctor thought further operations were unnecessary. At this stage, he usually assessed the main differences between the business partners, and which areas should be highlighted when it came to the fake assault. This time he believed it was the right side of the face. Though they had become almost indistinguishable from each other, The Doctor always considered it necessary to pull the wool over people's eyes when it came to the whole personality. The assault meant that sand was sprinkled in the eyes of the relatives, and other personality changes were considered normal, if indeed they aroused any attention at all.

Starkaður's wounds had healed, but Solomon thought he still needed another three weeks to reach his full form, both physically and mentally. When this was over, Almar and Starkaður would live together for a time in the author's city centre apartment, which had now been enlarged, and begin to exchange roles. Before that happened, Almar would be given time to say goodbye to his friends and family, provided they did not suspect what was going on. In the second week, he was to travel to London to give a reading from *Bernhard Zero*, at which the assault would be staged, so he would use the first week to say goodbye to Hildur and Bjartur.

For this he rented the Writers' Union cottage at Eyrarbakki, and invited them to come and stay for Easter. Before the trip he was very nervous, wanted everything to be perfect and for them to be happy when he took his leave of them. Starkaður recommended that he take some board games along, and download family movies for them to watch. He also asked him to bring a camera, and promised that he would have photos of him and Bjartur framed. Starkaður bought a necklace with stones based on the couple's astrological signs that Almar could give Hildur. When the author returned, Starkaður read the diaries with excitement.

April 22, 2011 Norðurbær

I took Bjartur down to the old pier to look for the seal we saw here last year, but it was nowhere to be seen. Bjartur thought the breakwater was so impressive that it could easily be lengthened until it reached America. Said hopefully that then we could all live in the same country. I recalled the story of the father who built a bridge across the river of youth so his son could grow up. For me that's as feasible as extending the breakwater at Eyrarbakki harbour over to America. And yet I'm succeeding with it in my own way.

I had the new camera with me and was constantly snapping. Hildur told me to stop, and hid the camera, but I found it again. I thought every moment was so precious that I had to capture it and scrutinise it immediately on the screen. I don't understand the compulsion to see my son in my camera's memory even though he's by my side. It's not as though I can take the camera with me where I'm going. It's more like I'm heading into the picture myself. Maybe that's it. I'm going into the picture, to him.

On the beach, Bjartur dug a hole in the sand which he got into, and then shovelled the sand together until he was half submerged. He was going to have trouble getting out of it. I thought of analogies like being buried under the sands of time, that sometimes in life one must work hard to dig oneself out of some trouble one had got oneself into, and that wasn't always much fun. But I didn't say anything. Just took his photo as he tried to free himself, laughing.

April 25th, 2011 Norðurbær Night

When Bjartur had gone to sleep, we left my phone on his bedside table, took Hildur's phone with us and strolled up to the Red House restaurant, where I bought her dessert. At the cottage, she had cooked my favourite lasagne. As we ate she said she didn't understand our relationship any more. How I could be so kindly disposed towards her now, quite out of the blue. Her lipstick left a red half-moon on the cup and I watched to see if it would break at the next sip, but it didn't happen. Soon the cup was empty. She stared down at it, head bowed, then refilled it, and scratched her nose, probably because of the evaporated moisture that had settled on it. Looked up and continued to talk. I missed what she was saying because I was remembering conversations I'd had with Solomon about dreams.

'Do you hear what I'm saying, Almar?'

'Sorry, I was dreaming for a minute.'

'I'm saying...'

She leaned across the table and whispered:

'It's not normal to live without sex. I mean, I'm invited out. What am I supposed to do with my time? Stay at home all evening and watch old episodes of Friends? *Emily has started to drag me out*

to the bar after work on Fridays, and there I meet men who want to take me out to dinner. I mean, one night I came home with three business cards from very nice men. I don't really want to go out with any of them. But Almar, eventually I will have to accept some of these invitations.

'I know that you can't sleep with me anymore, but if you were at home we would at least keep each other company. But no, that's not an option. Things between us have been really idiotic for a long time now... sometimes you send me such strange emails... almost like you were two different people... and now Bjartur is so happy to have us both around that he's over the moon with joy...'

I had fallen into such a deep silence that I felt as though the teacup had stuck in my mouth. Before she began to cry, I asked for the bill and took her outside. We walked down to the breakwater and watched the waves. That was how I was going to say goodbye to her. Watch the waves while I held her curving body. She had stopped talking and leaned her head on me as we walked. I whispered that I understood what she meant. This couldn't go on any longer. It had to come to an end. I said that no one deserved such a wonderful woman who waited for him even though he had not made her any promises. But now I was going to make one. I said that the extension of the apartment was complete, and invited her to come for a weekend in early June to see it when I had settled in. I would invite her to a romantic dinner, and the cherry on the cake: I promised sex.

She stopped and looked at me searchingly.

'Why then? Why not just now, tonight? Bjartur's asleep. He's so tired after today not even an earthquake would wake him.'

165

She was right, but I was sure that I wouldn't be able to make it. I put my hand on her hair that lay across her lips, asked if she could tolerate this strange situation of ours until June.

'I know it's a lot to ask. But I beg you. Whatever was bothering me, I feel I'm getting over it. I don't want to take a chance on offering something I can't live up to. I did enough of that abroad. But I know in my heart that I can fulfil this promise; and I yearn to do this for us. Then, after that I would want to see if I could come back to New York. Or do something else you agreed to. See if we can't resume a serious relationship again. Become a real family, like we were.'

She looked at me, at a loss, until her eyes grew moist. Gripped the necklace with our stones, the one I gave her on the first night. Held it so tightly that I was afraid the chain would break. I gathered the tears with my lips. As we embraced I felt I had the best and most faithful wife one could imagine.

The injuries after the alleged assault on Almar in London were induced in such a way that he was put under general anaesthetic in a hospital bed but woke up fifteen hours later in an independent clinic with fractured ribs and a swelling in the right-hand side of his face. A small news item appeared in the press to the effect that the author Almar Logi Almarsson had been the object of a motiveless assault on the way back to his Bloomsbury hotel in the early hours of Saturday morning and had received a head injury and concussion. At present, he was confined to bed, but he was still determined he would be able to get up and take charge of the reading he had arranged to hold at Café Súfistinn on Thursday May 5. There he planned to make a presentation to the Dream Club in honour of the publication of a dream collection by the club's founding member, Dr. Guðni Bjarnason.

Dr. Epstein said that when it came to the friendly takeover, perspicacious friends like Almar's buddies in the Dream Club most often created the main problem. They sometimes asked uncomfortable questions. A partner was an issue that had to be resolved, because if the partner saw no difference after the takeover, the doubts of others would not easily take hold. The partner could also be a manageable problem because in some cases love was blind. A partner readily ceased to see the person closest to them with complete clarity and began to experience them as a mood in their own emotional life. People did not deny parts of themselves so easily. If it were possible to create a situation where the reputation buyer and Hildur slept together, she would hardly ask fundamental questions afterwards. If things were managed correctly, a long period of sexual abstinence might help the takeover, because it was a situation to which she was very eager to put an end. As always, much effort would be needed to prepare the circumstances surrounding this crucial process.

With close friends, on the other hand, there was no way of dealing with a misleading action like an intense lovers' rendezvous. An infraction of the norm like a crude assault on the reputation seller might help, but sometimes it was not enough. When Solomon considered that an especially perceptive friend like Dr. Guðni was involved, other stricter measures were needed. Then it would be best to stage an event that would lead to mutual hostility. For as they say: if anything blinds more than love, it is hatred.

The question of whether the reputation buyer would then cultivate this artificial hatred and not let the friends into his life, was up to him. But at the peak of the traffic, when the takeover was at its most sensitive, it would be necessary to resort to this tactic. Though one would have to tread carefully, so that the hostility did not go to the core, the quality of the reputation.

In the aftermath of his coded farewell at the Dream Club reading, which was well attended, Almar had a colleague of his make a phone call to a critic who was due to talk about Dr. Guðni's recently published collection of dreams. During the call the colleague let it be known that the dreams had been stolen from an old dream collection of Almar's, as had many of the ideas in the essays that accompanied the book. Following this, a Sunday newspaper published an interview with Guðni, the author of *The Naked Suitor*, in which this alleged plagiarism was discussed. As he lay on a bunk in the loft of the warehouse, Starkaður read:

...The members and I don't know what may have induced our old dream friend to assert this, for I understand that he is the source of the rumour. Indeed, I thought he was a bit different from his usual self at the reading he gave at Café Súfistinn. Frankly, one had the impression that he might have received a mild brain injury in the assault he suffered in London a few days earlier. I expect that this was also accompanied by psychological shock. In time he will recover, and hopefully we shall go back to discussing dreams. I hope from the bottom of my heart that this is so, for what is happening to society if the members of a small unit like the Dream Club can't even show solidarity...

Solomon was delighted at the spread of public speculation that Almar's personality had been damaged as a result of the assault. Such publicity created a sympathetic atmosphere, which the friendly takeover would need when it came to the most sensitive stage: the cohabitation of reputation seller and reputation buyer, and the friendly takeover itself.

20

After more than six months indoors, Starkaður was relieved to escape from the draughty warehouse in Grindavík and move into Almar's place downtown. It was an old wooden building that had become somewhat grander after the attic flat had spread out over the whole extent of the roof. There they lived together in peace and harmony like twin brothers and took turns going out to attend to the author's business. Starkaður's first official task in his new role was going to the grocery on the corner. There he chatted with the old woman at the checkout about the newspaper headlines that were frequently about matters related to the economic crisis. They had even gone outside for a smoke and specifically discussed the case of Starkaður Levi, which had much prominence in the media because of the ongoing search for him. At home Starkaður had taken over Almar's email and Internet, though the author still read the text over to check it. When the phone rang, they both listened to the callers but took turns at answering them.

A great deal of money had gone into refurbishing the apartment, but the old-fashioned style made the building's grand appearance seem perfectly natural. In the author's office Dr. Epstein, had installed a work studio for Rita, who was to be the Firm's representative in the apartment for the crucial moments with Hildur. Since the apartment was small, the studio had to be thoroughly soundproofed. In the work room, there was a tall, specially designed ottoman sofa with a large drawer that could be locked from inside. There Starkaður and Rita were to wait while Almar showed his wife the apartment after the change. The Doctor himself planned to monitor developments on television screens in the warehouse. Twelve hidden cameras had been set up so that nothing would escape him. Since all communications with Hildur were in Icelandic, Almar and Starkaður had to take turns translating for Rita and The Doctor when they were in the work room.

At supper time Starkaður cooked one of his pasta dishes and taught Almar how to bake his hallmark, an apple cake with cinnamon. The Doctor had laid particular emphasis on the cake, and said, smiling, that no one who was able to make a good apple cake could be all bad. The cake was important for the dinner with Hildur. She was expected to arrive from New York on Friday, June 3 and for dinner the following evening. Then on the Sunday she would fly back home.

Starkaður must have had some problems with the cake, because neither of them took more than one mouthful of it. Almar sat by the window and looked out at the street. He had always dreamed of the apartment reaching all the way to the eaves so he could observe the downtown life. Starkaður sat in the shadow of the parlour, one leg dangling, and watching the back of Almar's head. The author wore military trousers, a crumpled, loose brown shirt, a half-buttoned white sweater and an amber-coloured kerchief in a tangle around his neck. Starkaður found that the hardest thing was to get used to nearly always wearing a kerchief. They both had the same fit clothes, except that Almar's trousers were slightly too short on Starkaður. In spite of his ordinary bohemian uniform, the author appeared to be enclosed in a vanishing world. As long as he did not have to look at him too long, buried in his own version of unbreakable silence, Starkaður felt a strange affection for him. The longer the silence lasted, the more relaxed Almar became, while Starkaður became more and more irritable.

Starkaður briefly turned on the television news with

the remote control and heard the announcer talk about Glitnir Bank, which had been robbed from the inside, and the disappearance of Starkaður Levi. A search had been made at his home, without revealing any evidence of his present whereabouts. Starkaður turned the set off before the news item was over. Looked back at Almar and then down at the identical clothes he himself was wearing. If he did not say something soon he would fall prey to silence, like the author. That far he was not prepared to go for a new reputation.

'When I was on the notorious board of the bank's directors, the most memorable thing I did had nothing to do with business intrigues. Nothing at all.'

Almar did not react to these words. Accustomed to this, Starkaður continued:

'The most memorable thing I did was on the night I went down to the basement to check the deposit boxes that had come from the old bank. The forgotten deposit boxes of deceased individuals that could not be touched because of strict regulations aroused my curiosity as soon as I heard about them. I couldn't rest until I'd fathomed how to get hold of them. Even though I was on the board of directors I had to use all my ingenuity to get time undisturbed in the basement. Indeed, it was such a hassle figuring out the codes and getting copies of the keys that this was the only time I have had the experience of being a bank robber, as some people call me today. Though, remarkably enough, I wasn't looking for money. Imagine that. No, I was searching for something, but didn't know what it was. As an author, you must know that feeling.'

'So did you get into them?'

Starkaður was startled to receive a response.

'The deposit boxes, you mean? Yes, I did.'

'What did you find?'

'What did I find? It's quite a story. In the first box, there was an orange photo album and a colourful bundle of letters. I thought it was rather boring until I looked at the letters. There were various loose items in them, rolls of obsolete banknotes, locks of fair hair, falcon feathers, dried flowers that crumbled to the touch. But it was the subject-matter of the letters that awoke my interest. The box's owner had a secret family in Scotland that he visited only when he was on what his family here in Iceland believed to be a business trip.'

'A secret family?'

'Yes, he was a married man over here when he met a poor cleaning maid at the hotel he stayed at in Glasgow. To be completely safe, he introduced himself as a Norwegian right from the start. He had learned Norwegian when he lived in Tromsø for a time with his parents. As fortune would have it, he kept the cleaning woman for thirty years and had two daughters by her, both of whom thought their father was from Tromsø in Norway. Under a false name I managed to trace the older sister, Anna, on Facebook. She said that after her father stopped visiting without warning, she and her sister had gone to Tromsø to look for him and other relatives. They had found an old man called Ole, who was sure that his recently deceased cousin had been their father. Surviving relatives of this man wanted nothing to do with the sisters. They said that their father had never been to Glasgow. This was something that Ole insisted angrily was a most blatant lie – the father had been there many times.'

Starkaður laughed at his own story, and gazed smilingly at Almar's back.

'Anna said they were actually still in contact with Ole and his family. But they didn't know what had happened to their father. They were just sure he was alive. Ridiculous,

173

isn't it? Just shows how compartmentalized life can be. Like those pictures by that fellow who painted those bent chests of drawers in the desert.'

'Salvador Dali.'

'Yes, Dali. In the second box, there was a diamond necklace and a will that had clearly not been fully followed. In the last box, I peeked into there was a poetry manuscript. The title was *Passwords*. I still have it in a Swiss bank vault. They were erotic poems. What do you think the password was? Of course, it was...'

'Orgasm, I expect. Isn't that the trend nowadays? The password to the religion of happiness?'

Many things flew through Starkaður's mind, but as soon as Almar began to speak he bit his tongue. He would have enough time to unburden his heart. For a while he toyed with the TV remote control, but then laid it aside and put on one of Almar's CDs. Rodrigo's guitar concerto. The sad music sounded until he could not sit still any longer, got up, walked into the kitchen which was connected with the parlour and began to select ingredients for the apple cake. As usual, he beckoned to Almar to come and bake it, then he would copy him, step by step. While the author was mixing the dough in the bowl lugubriously, he said:

'Speaking of the password.'

Starkaður repositioned himself, took the brand new mixer and moved his hand slowly with the same leisurely movement as the author.

'Orgasm, you mean?'

'Yes'.

'What about it?'

'If you want her to have it.'

'Who?'

174

'Your wife.'

'Hildur?'

'If you want her to have it.'

'Yes.'

'Then go easy on the fuss.'

'Okay.'

'Begin by warming her up with compliments and teasing. Maybe you can practice some gymnastics, there at the start. But when it comes down to it, the thing is just to vanish. Not a word. Not a glance. Feel the wave-like movements between the thighs. Not with the weight of your whole body, but just with your hips. She will get more aroused if she finds that you are relaxed, as though what you're doing is the most natural thing. Remember to keep quiet and let her moans fill the room. Feel the waves come and grab you naturally as if you were being rocked at low tide. Meanwhile look over her shoulder so she can't see your face. After a few minutes, she will wash ashore like the most beautiful mermaid – she is an absolute enchantress at that.'

Almar licked dough from his fingers and continued:

'When she's lying there, shiny in the sand, you can make yourself noticeable again. Even get up to some tricks. But so that she gets satisfaction again, you have to vanish for her with this method. If you learn this, she can have one orgasm after another all night– something she will rub your nose in, bragging; I came four times, what about you?'

Starkaður had never considered sex that focused on the woman's orgasm, and looked thoughtfully at Almar slice apples.

'Vanish? I thought the important thing was to be present. Why vanish like that?'

'I don't know, that's just how it is with Hildur. Maybe

she needs a steady, silent wave rhythm to get to a certain place in her mind. Up in some ancient tower in the unconscious where she has a view of her dreams and can let herself fall out and soar in the sun-red silken veils of femininity. What do I know.'

Starkaður sliced apples, wondering about the big evening that lay ahead, and especially about what The Doctor had said about Hildur really wanting a man who was an 'underdog'. He implied that this was something Almar had never realised. While growing up and later at her job she had been surrounded by alpha males, but fell for Almar's helplessness. His eyes were always slightly distant, as if he were looking beyond this world, and was to some extent vulnerable in it. Yet sometimes he could be very manly without knowing it. She needed these perpetual contrasts to find him attractive. He recommended that if Starkaður were nervous, shy or insecure, he should let it be seen. That kind of thing would only help. If he was too confident she would interpret it as impertinence rather than eroticism, feel she was at a family gathering or a meeting at work, and stiffen up.

For several weeks Starkaður had studied pictures of Hildur before he went to sleep, and reflected that he and Almar had similar tastes in women. Now he could clearly picture her on the sofa, the warm brown eyes, the determined mouth, the attractive body. But he could not imagine what their relationship was like. All he saw was him kissing her, and then one thing led to another. He had forgotten himself in musing, and was startled when Almar put the cake in the oven and the door closed. He still had a great deal to do. Rather than asking yet again how to do it, he tried to patch the cake together from what he could decipher of the remains on the table.

'She got pregnant right after you slept together for the

first time, didn't she?'

'Yes.'

'But there was something about the miscarriage I didn't understand. You were in Visby on Gotland, finishing a book. She was already two months pregnant when this happened. But she couldn't reach you because you didn't have a phone.'

'I had a dream.'

'The one with the bug.'

'Maybe. What was it about?

'She was calling out to you but was trapped in another room, wasn't she?'

'Sounds familiar.'

Starkaður quickly recounted the dream:

'You called out to her through the door, asked what she was doing. She answered, shaken, that she had heard something alive in the cupboard, and had opened it. And did you find anything? you asked. Yes, I found an insect. And what was it doing? you asked.'

Almar stopped him, thought for a moment, and continued:

'When she answered in one impassioned word, it was like a dam bursting: Nothing! Then came a waterfall of tears which I could still hear when I woke up. I was drenched in sweat and feeling sick to my stomach. I knew immediately that this was an important dream.'

Starkaður sprinkled cinnamon on the cake, put it in the oven and looked at Almar, who seemed pensive.

'Yes, exactly. But that's all that's in the diary. Which is odd, because you often reflect on dreams that are in no way unusual.'

'Was there nothing about it?'

'Not a word.'

'It's probably because I knew what it meant when I wrote it, and rushed out after that.'

'What did it mean?'

'Her being on the other side of a wall meant she was in another country. The cupboard was the womb, the insect was the foetus. The insect not doing anything meant that the foetus was dead. When I realised that I ran down to a petrol station and called her from the coin-box. By then she had been trying to reach me for three days.'

The Rodrigo CD was finished. From the street came rap music and the singing of young people on their way out on the town. When they emerged from the oven, the cakes were very different from each other. One had risen majestically, but the other had stuck to the bottom. When the street grew quieter, Almar sat at the window again and Starkaður in the armchair in the parlour. They smoked in synchronisation. Starkaður looked back at the author until he heard him say:

'Once when I was alone with Bjartur at Eyrarbakki, I was suddenly surprised to hear him talking about his brother. I asked who he this was. He found it odd that I didn't know. He was, of course, talking about his brother who died. He had made up a lot of ideas about the foetus that never became a child. He also longed for siblings, and for Hildur to have more children. Perhaps that, in conjunction with other things, led to the fact that I stopped being able to sleep with her. I don't understand why people feel bound to bring more children into this world. Children who grow up and become part of a herd of adults who know nothing about what they are, what they are doing or where they are going.'

21

To be on the safe side, Starkaður and Rita got into the linen drawer of the sofa in the work studio five minutes before Hildur was due to arrive for dinner. There was a mattress in the drawer, as the sofa was expandable to a double bed. Starkaður lay behind Rita; the curly hairs of her ponytail irritated his nose. She had arrived early, dressed provocatively, something The Doctor had insisted on. To create the right attitude in Starkaður for Hildur's arrival, he said. She had swung her hips as she stepped lightly in high heels and fishnet tights and a red skirt, helping to lay the table, pick out suitable CDs, dim the lights and light the candles. Finally, she put an erotic movie in the player, in case there would not be enough romance in the air. In the darkness of the drawer Starkaður smelled Rita's scent and listened to her slow breathing. They heard the door open: Almar was telling Hildur about the new pictures on the walls – they were of doubles, he said. Starkaður used the opportunity to secretly put his hand on Rita's hips and check the size of the mesh in her pantyhose. The mesh was wide enough for him to get his fingertips through and examine the rigidness of her skin. He knew that she would not move while voices rang in the room, and listened to her breathing grow faster. Suddenly there was a loud rasping sound from the boards above them, and Starkaður jerked his hand towards him, bumping his head on the base of the sofa. Hildur had flung herself on the sofa, swaying to and fro so that the boards creaked. They heard her cheerful voice:

'So now you can always change the den into a guest room?'

Almar replied:

'Yes, or just lie down for a while and read the manuscript if I'm stuck.'

'Or widen the sofa and ask me to help you. I can feel that the bottom is made with stress in mind.'

'Or that, yes. Though it would be more help with finding happiness than with finishing the book.'

'What's the difference?'

They heard Hildur stand up, and waited for the strain on the inner lock of the drawer when she tried to open it. But that did not happen. The voices drifted away and the door of the room closed. Rita pushed away Starkaður's hand, which was on her hips, and opened the drawer. They sat down at the desk, started the computer and watched the couple on the screen.

On her arrival Rita had tested the cameras and checked that they worked, both on the computer and with Dr. Epstein in the warehouse. She also tested the transmitters that the business partners had in their ears. The Doctor considered them necessary so he could whisper advice to them if they got into a dilemma, and to be able to indicate when they ought to exchange the role of host.

If all went according to plan, Almar was to have dinner with her, but then when Hildur felt at ease, he would clear the table and Starkaður would bring in the dessert. If everything worked out, the reputation buyer was to spend the evening with her thereafter. Otherwise they would put Almar back in as needed until Starkaður had control of the situation.

As they watched the couple on the screen, it troubled Starkaður to hear Rita's breathing in the earpiece. Hildur wore a black dress, and a black hair-band. Starkaður thought she looked elegant, but Rita was worried that she looked as if she were at a funeral. She was not dressed for a lovers' rendezvous and that she was not wearing the necklace that Almar had given her at Eyrarbakki when they made the date did not give her a good feeling. She said they would have to do something drastic. Out of the blue, she turned to Starkaður, who was scratching his ear, and gave him a warm kiss. Starkaður was startled, but when he had recovered and was about to embrace her she pushed him firmly away and pointed to the screen. Told him sternly to watch with close attention.

At first the atmosphere between the couple at dinner was good, though Almar looked rather serious. They reminisced about their first meeting, and many memorable events and places where they had made love. Starkaður found it reassuring to know the story behind all the places they mentioned, the beach at Eyrarbakki, the camping trip to Búðir, the hotel in Berlin on their honeymoon. Rita whispered to Almar to stick to romantic memories. The food was ready and there was a gleam in Hildur's eyes when she looked at her husband. Rita whispered to Starkaður that this was a romantic silence, stroking his thigh expectantly. At the same moment Hildur put her hand on Almar's thigh. Rita gazed at Starkaður confidently. Contact with his wife seemed to make the author relax and be himself. He held the empty glass close to him and stared ahead, with glazed eyes. He began a monologue for an interested listener whom only he saw:

'And speaking of memories, it gets to the point where one shuts one's eyes and then that's the last thing one sees. Whether one remembers it for a while behind one's eyelids, just before everything's wiped out, no one knows. But perhaps that memory is the last thing one sees, and it's a window into the soul. Everything in one's mind wants to connect to the last memory, as if it were a famous film star on the red carpet of consciousness. The mind's safety gates burst and a mass of suppressed memories rushes after the falling film star at the premiere of death. On the screen appears the soul's last attempt to endow all this with meaning. Perhaps it's a good movie, or perhaps it isn't. No one knows, for it gets no reviews in the papers next day. All the critics are dead.'

While Almar whispered this gloomy speech, Rita jumped to her feet and, grabbing the microphone, told him firmly to change the subject. Immersed in his own thoughts, he did not seem to hear, and continued to destroy the romantic atmosphere as if that were the principal aim of the evening:

'But the last thing I see will probably be my own face watching me disappear. It could even happen this week. Yes, at 4 pm on Tuesday, June 7, for example. It's a suitable metaphor, isn't it? To leave life when others are leaving their workplace to go home?'

The amorous flush that had come to Hildur's face after they reminisced about their courtship and early years together over two bottles of red wine was completely gone. The only bright thing in her gloom was that her drinking speed had increased by half, and she was now opening the third bottle. Rita hissed into the microphone:

'Stand up, Almar, at once, and apologise. Say that you oughtn't to be talking about boring things, and now we've arrived at the aspect of your character she fell for at the beginning: the apple cake! Tell her to take a bottle and glasses into the sofa while you fetch the cake!'

Almar woke with a start as from a bad dream, and mechanically obeyed the wishes of the voice in his ear. Rita was furious, and had to suppress a scream when he made his way in, but as soon as he had got there and closed up behind him, she looked at him more considerately. She made him lie on the bed, caressed his forehead and gave him some whisky. On the computer screen it could be seen that Hildur seemed to be paralysed after the melancholy speech. They zoomed into her face. Her eyes were moist, the eyeliner had formed black tears on her left cheek. For the third time in a short period she applied her lipstick. The rim of her glass was red all round. Rita whispered that she had seen this same sad look when Hildur, at a New York restaurant, had told her in a drunk voice what a loser her husband could be. Soon after that she had vanished. She looked at Almar, who hid his face in his hands, groaning.

'We can't send him in like that.'

She had another look at the screen:

'And we can't make her wait because then she'll just leave. Or start looking for him in the apartment, and we'll all be in trouble.'

She gazed at Starkaður. He looked as though he were watching an exciting movie.

'Now you're going to be put to the test.'

22

When Starkaður brought in the apple cake, Hildur sat with her feet tucked under her, looking like a drowsy mermaid. Her reaction upon seeing him was decisive. Instinctively she moved further away from him on the sofa, then quickly stood up and smoothed her dress along her legs.

'Something wrong?' Starkaður asked, putting the cake on the table.

'Wrong? No, no.'

She stared at him as if something magnificent was coming. He smiled teasingly

'You got up quickly enough.'

'Did I, now?'

'Yes. But now that you're on your feet, lazybones, perhaps you can help me with the cream and the plates. I'm going to lay the table.'

Suddenly she seemed to have turned into a statue, and had to exert herself in order to move. She managed to free herself from her straitjacket, and followed him reluctantly to the kitchen.

Starkaður turned his back to her and stirred the bowl of cream, even though it was already whipped.

'Seriously, is something wrong, darling?'

'No, not at all. I was merely surprised to see how quickly you recovered your composure. You went so dreadfully gloomy all of a sudden earlier. I've often seen you down in the mouth, but never like that. When you looked at me I felt you were looking into the face of death itself. It wasn't exactly a very romantic feeling.'

'Yes, no, sorry, you misunderstood me, Hildur. I forgot to tell you that I was reciting part of a book I'm writing. It's always best to try things out on people directly. Have you completely forgotten my little ways?'

'No, I don't think so. I don't remember you trying out your writing like that before. I'd like to stick to the old way of reading the manuscript. Also, it might be nice to forget about literature in the few moments we have together.'

'You're right, I see it now. Once again, I'm sorry.'

Throughout the conversation Starkaður had had his back turned to her, but now felt that this would not do much longer. On the counter next to the refrigerator was a bottle of schnapps he and Almar had had some of the night before, but was not intended for Hildur. He opened the glass cabinet, took out two shot glasses and filled them to the brim. When he turned around with a sudden gesture, some of the liquid spilled over her. She looked down at her front, which was covered in drops. When she looked up there was a silent smile on her lips as she stared at him in the half light. Slowly she raised her right hand towards his cheek as if to touch the wound and check if he was real. Starkaður watched blankly as the delicate fingers with their painted red nails approached his face, felt like nibbling them. Before she could touch him he handed her a glass:

'Cheers!'

He drained his glass. Hildur seemed unable to take her eyes off him, but at last followed his example and knocked her glass back. Starkaður rushed into the room with plates, set the table and flopped down in the armchair. She followed him at a distance, put the cream bowl on the table, sat down on the sofa and picked up the cake knife. Examined it from head to toe, cut the cake in silence and put some on his plate. Starkaður found it hard to sit still, and felt instinctively in his pocket for cigarettes. He lit one, and blew smoke over the table.

'Smoking indoors? You always used to go down to the front steps to smoke.'

'Yes, no, not at all, or yes, but really only when I'm tense.'

'Tense, are you? Why?'

Starkaður was about to justify himself, but bit his lower lip. He remembered that Almar was often silent, even when he was spoken to. In the earpiece, he heard Solomon remind him to flow with his own emotions and acknowledge them until the aura around him was at its most truthful. He should float on his emotions, such as those that surrounded the cake.

'I'm excited because of the apple cake. I was afraid you wouldn't like it.'

Hildur took the plate, leaned back in the sofa and had a mouthful. She did not take her eyes off Starkaður. Ate half of the slice while she looked him up and down.

'You're an absolute freak, Almar, do you know that?'

'How do you like it?'

'Do you want an honest answer?'

Her teasing voice helped Starkaður to get the feeling that they knew each other.

'An honest answer? Yes, if something like that exists.'

'It does, Almar. And, it's ... it's ... different. Really different. I don't know what to think about it. You are obviously not going to get any, since you use your plate as an ashtray. Did you put roofie in it? I feel there's something a bit rapey about you suddenly. The way you look at me is repulsive. Remember, we know each other rather well. For example, you were there when our son Bjartur was born. Hello, Almar, does that ring any bells?'

Starkaður had missed what she said. He had his eyes on her thighs. She was rocking them slowly apart and together, seemingly without noticing. He lit another cigarette, dropping the match on the floor instead of throwing it on the plate.

'There's no need to get all tensed up because of an apple cake. Watch carefully, I'm eating it. Mmmmm, it's ...'

Hildur stuck out her tongue and licked the cream off the spoon. Starkaður gazed open-mouthed at the pink tongue.

'Are you sure there isn't anything else that makes you tense?'

'It's not impossible.'

The Doctor whispered in his ear that he should make the tension fit the promise Almar had made when they last met:

'Perhaps something I promised you.'

'Promised?'

'When we walked along the beach at Eyrarbakki.'

'That was small talk. There's no pressure.'

'Really?'

'No, no, no pressure. It's just something I've been dreaming about for just over two years and made a trip all the way from New York for. You know, it's recently become a fantasy about losing my virginity. Don't tell anyone.'

Starkaður waited for The Doctor to guide him forward through the conversation, but now he said not a word. The silence was becoming too long, so he said the first thing that came into his mind:

'And you are saying that *I'm* a freak?'

She gave him a stern look.

'It's highly contagious. Don't you remember that I always get really ridiculous when I'm with you. Why do you think I started with you, idiot?'

Hildur suddenly gave him such a beautiful smile that he felt a tickling deep in his chest. Despite all the movie watching he had never seen her look as sincere as she did now. He wanted to say something clever, but all he could think of was to say that he was indeed a rapist, the most devious one to date. So devious that he had even fooled himself out of his own life until he landed in her delightful company. He found that it paid not to open his mouth as things stood, blindly fumbled for the remote control and turned on the TV. For a few moments they watched the scene on the screen. Hildur's expression became increasingly strange, and she blushed to the roots of her hair:

'You're crazy, Almar. In the middle of a cake party you put on a hard core movie about a lady with, what's this, twins in a bed? What's that on the bedside table? A birthday cake? And the men with gilt ribbons around their necks. Are they supposed to be giving themselves as birthday presents? Is that what you watch when you could be at home in bed with me?'

She looked at him. The amorous flush had risen to her cheeks again.

'You're extremely stupid, do you know that?'

'Yes, I surely do. And not only that. As you can see, I'm a rapist.'

Hildur laughed. Put her hand on the sofa beside her:

'Come here, my crazy birthday rapist.'

Starkaður stubbed out his cigarette and moved over to her without touching her. She ran her eyes down him:

'Is that what I think it is? Is something down there pleased to see me?'

She kissed him and stroked her body against him.

'If that's the new summer fashion, I rather like it.'

He felt like touching her but restrained himself,

following The Doctor's advice to let her keep the initiative since she had taken it. Her hands went down, undid his fly, and one of them crept inside.

'Ooh la la,' she said, smiling.

Starkaður put his head on her shoulder and breathed in the smell of her hair while she stroked him. Before he knew it, he had come. Hildur watched amazed as the wet stain spread on his trousers, and had fits of laughter. When he was about to leap to his feet, she held on to him and kissed him:

'Sorry, I didn't mean to laugh at you. This is a much more positive problem.'

She looked at her watch.

'And the night is young. We can still make the best of it. Oops, all finished, ha ha, you're unique, Almar, I'm so glad I waited for you. Ha ha, sorry, I'm not laughing. The emotions are flying in all directions with you now, like in the old days. Eroticism, sorrow, crippling fear. Like when you brought your phenomenal cake into the parlour. Suddenly I was so scared. Of a new beginning, maybe, or hopes for the future, perhaps it was a fear of losing you again in the darkness...'

In the midst of all the playacting, the unexpected and very real orgasm had knocked Starkaður off balance, and suddenly everything seemed to him unreal. At one moment, he wanted to put his arms round Hildur and enjoy the highly-charged lovers' bickering, but at another he wanted to silence her and push her away from him. When there was a squeaking sound in his throat that he did not recognize, he put his hand to his mouth and bit the back of his hand. In his ear, he heard The Doctor call firmly:

'Don't let her see your face! Stand up and say that you need to clean yourself up in the bathroom!'

Starkaður tore himself away from her and did as the

voice commanded. He stormed through the kitchen along to the den, where he surprised Almar and Rita: the door was unlocked and they were both sitting at the desk together. Almar's left hand rested on the hem of Rita's skirt, which rode high on her thigh. They had clearly not been paying much attention to the screen, as Rita demanded an immediate explanation of his arrival. When she had realised the situation she told Almar to go into the bathroom, wet his trousers as if he had been cleaning them and take over until Starkaður was ready again.

After three quarters of an hour Starkaður had recovered, and Rita called Almar back in. He looked pretty shattered but had kept his wife laughing most of the time by making fun of his own performance during sex.

Shortly after Starkaður vanished into the sofa, he and Hildur tried again, and this time got further, but once again it ended with Hildur in fits of laughter. Late at night in the bedroom, when Almar and Rita had left the apartment and had travelled south for the meeting in the warehouse in Grindavík, Hildur had her first orgasm in two years and seven months. Through her powerful moans one could hear The Doctor clapping, before he said a curt goodbye and reminded them that they were to meet at the airport the following day.

23

The Small Firm rented two suites overlooking the harbour district of Amsterdam, where on the final evening of the takeover they all sat together at a festive dinner in Almar and Starkaður's suite. Dr. Epstein stood up in his finest suit and said that this had been his most successful takeover to date, thanks to the partners. He proposed a toast to them. He also spoke about Stoicism, considered the classical serenity of Marcus Aurelius regarding death, a subject that Almar was able to pick up in his speech. Starkaður could not remember anything of those discussions except that they had quoted from *Julius Caesar*. The emperor was supposed to have said something the night before he was killed to the effect that he had seen a friend of his die a so-called natural death, and that it had been the cruellest mortal struggle he had ever witnessed. After that he wished only that when his time came he would meet with a sudden end. The Doctor also talked about sacrifice as the ancient basis of society, asserting that the self-sacrifice of the fit was always a sign that society was healthy. He said that a positive or negative ending to life had an effect on the living. A good life that ended badly, in an ugly suicide, for example, cast too much of a shadow on the positive things that such a life had produced. His task was to create a path from the core of the best, who had given their all, had thought their way out of the world but were trapped in life, a path into the very heart of society. That path was sacrifice, the ultimate gift of life. The process was based on the same principle that the story of the Passion in the New Testament dealt with, though in a rather different way. The friendly takeover was not about divine sacrifice, but rather about the human form of it that dwells deep down in those who love the world more than themselves and want to end their lives by transforming their love into society. This idea could also be seen in the Old Testament's Book of Judges, in the story of the chieftain Jephthah and his only daughter who gladly died as a burnt offering after God ensured his victory over Ammon.

Starkaður had heard most of this before. For some reason, he could not work out, he got a bad taste in his mouth.

And then, with the same sincere emotion, the same passionate interest, they discussed the food.

Starkaður could not believe his ears. He found it nightmarish that at this moment they could all sit together like old colleagues, drink toasts with good wine, and chat about the food. Was it appropriate to talk about it, as things stood? Didn't food exist to sustain life? Solomon raised his glass, looked into it searchingly, and said:

'We're drinking the best wine in the hotel. It's superb, as we all feel. But there are limits to how good wine can be. Its quality depends on who one drinks it with and under what circumstances. All circumstances and the quality of all material things are subject to limits. No matter how beautiful the surroundings, how good the people, or how good the wine in one's glass, the result is always limited. And yet people pursue this as though it concealed limitless concepts like infinity and eternity. But there is only one thing that is possibly limitless in human existence, and that is the spirit.'

Almar listened to him with attention, and after a short pause added:

'Since man doesn't live by bread alone, food criticism can never become a science. The field can't be defined, so scientific food criticism, where the critic eats under grey, silent and neutral conditions, does not exist. When it does exist, man will have ceased to be human and the computers will have disposed not only of memory but also of the life of the soul.'

At this they smiled, with glasses raised. All except Starkaður.

The Doctor said:

'Indeed. Men instinctively associate an atmosphere with good times. The phenomenon of atmosphere conceals some irrational elements. First one may mention a semi-irrational phenomenon such as happiness. Then one may proceed to words like ecstasy, and end with terms like eternity, infinity, and those abstract words that are simply there, though it's doubtful if anyone can understand them, as it's impossible that they are backed up by experience.'

Starkaður thought of interjecting that the concept of death might be one of those words, out there in the atmosphere. But he controlled himself.

Almar watched Solomon with admiration, as though he understood exactly where he was going. Stood up with his glass raised, and continued merrily:

'You are mistaken, Doctor. Of course a concept like eternity can be understood.'

'I doubt it.'

'It's terribly simple.'

'Oh?'

'Yes, it's all so simple. A bird is a moment, the tree eternity. There is always a bird on the branch, but never the same one. In the autumn a thousand birds die in the woods, but you never mourn them. It's so simple. A face is the temporal, the wind against it the eternal. There is always a face against the wind, but never the same one. And eternity is the memory of a moment that one yearns to reclaim.'

'What kind of moment?'

'Like with one's son on the beach at Eyrarbakki.'

Starkaður recalled the photos of father and son on the beach, where the boy was half buried in sand. He thought of saying that it was quite possible to re-experience that moment. But The Doctor got in first:

'You mean that if one experiences an intense moment one wants to relive, one perceives that time as an insurmountable and invincible force. The feeling one derives from that experiment is then transferred to the concept of eternity, and one thereby thinks that one understands it.'

'One understands it because one has a feeling...'

Starkaður could not fathom what they were driving at, and had to exert all his energy not to stand up and shout at them to stop this nonsense. But he could not envisage what would come next. What he would do after silencing them. He stood up and excused himself. Went out on the balcony to smoke. Rita followed him. Starkaður felt somewhat pressured by her smiling stance. As if a steely discipline lay behind it. When they had lit their cigarettes and Starkaður looked across the city, he said:

'I don't understand how we can call this business when Almar is getting nothing out of it.'

'You don't understand that the merchandise Almar longs for most of all is death.'

Starkaður shook his head irritably.

'How can you talk about death as though it were some merchandise? Death is something we all get for free, isn't it?'

Rita gave him a look of exhaustion, as if she thought he was pretending to be naive about a subject they had discussed many times. She studied him searchingly, and then put her hand on the back of his and said:

'Almar doesn't want to jump off the building so his people will have to spend the rest of their days wiping the blood off the pavement around him. The death he longs for is clean bedlinen, a made up bed, which is suddenly empty when you've stepped away from it. His body doesn't even leave a mark on the sheets.'

Starkaður had twice blown smoke uncomprehendingly in her direction before she went on:

'Death is many-faceted, Starkaður. Almar doesn't long for death for its own sake, he longs to escape from life. He's not afraid of death, but he's afraid of leaving life in a way that hurts those whom he dearly loves. What we at the Firm are bringing him is a death that accords with his own wishes. No one has control of death, but Almar is getting the death of his own choice. He is getting a death that releases him from the complex life that weighs on us in so many different ways. Almar is like a puppet on a string that breaks free and disappears from the stage. But then, when fate pulls the strings again, there is still a puppet that reacts. The puppet is you. Relatives happily applaud the puppet on stage with them, not realizing that right under their noses the greatest illusionary trick in the history of prestidigitation has just been performed.'

'So you're selling him his own death. That's an even cheekier business deal than the one I pulled off when I made my nation responsible for my debts several decades to come.'

'From a narrow-minded perspective, maybe. But it's all on you, you know.'

'Oh? How come?'

'You're the one who's paying. Because when Almar dies, you come to life, and when you die, he comes to life.'

'Doing business with the supernatural, you mean?'

'No, Starkaður. This is just a sophisticated deal, of

subjective value. Existential business, as Solomon calls it. Don't make this more complicated than it needs to be. You'll accomplish nothing but undue distress.'

Rita flicked her cigarette butt off the balcony and went inside. Through the window Starkaður watched her sit down smiling at the table beside Almar. After demonstratively applying her lipstick with theatrical gestures, she put her hand around his neck and gave him a smacking kiss on the cheek.

24

Dr. Epstein was in high spirits, and revealed far more about his life than Starkaður had expected him to. He talked about how he was looking forward to taking a sabbatical year with his wife, they were going to spend time with Clark and their grandchildren in the Caribbean. They were going on a sailing cruise there and around the Mediterranean. He talked about the grandchildren, and said that he hoped Rita would be luckier the next time she was pregnant. Then he would let her stop work and take care of the prospective child as his own grandson. He was going to expand on this, but Rita had begun to say "psst!" at almost everything he said. Starkaður had said more or less nothing all evening. Suddenly The Doctor staggered over to him, showed him a box of cigars and told him to follow him out to the balcony. Starkaður leaned on the balcony door with the intention of enjoying the peace and quiet, but Solomon towered over him, gripping him by the shoulder. When Solomon spoke, he breathed thick smoke into Starkaður's face:

'Of course, what you do tomorrow is none of my business, Starkaður. You have promised various good things, like showing respect to Arnar´s reputation, and being of more support to his family than he is. I trust you in this. In reality, you may do something quite different. But I trust you to try, at least. A person who wants to acquire a good reputation and is willing to take on a year's work to do so is not insane. He won't throw it away without warning when he finally receives it.

'Perhaps you think that because you've managed to get Hildur into bed it's all signed and sealed. I wish that it were so. But the thing is that she was a drunk, lovesick, sex-starved woman in a dimly-lit room with a man who was greatly interested in her. I hope you realize that these are very special circumstances. Very well, she has accepted your body as it is, as the body of her husband. That is something to build on. But if you think you have free access to her, you have another thing coming.

'I got Rita to obtain information about her, and according to my psychological assessment Hildur is a first-class wife, mother, employee and human being. She is probably too good for both you and for Almar, even though we got the best out of the two of you. And that means only one thing, my friend. You cannot endlessly fool around with her. She is a proud woman. You slipped into her personal space that night because she was making one final attempt to save the marriage. But be sure of one thing, Starkaður. If you choose to go to New York and try to adopt family life, a great and difficult task awaits you.

'You can bet on one thing: she's angry underneath. If she lets you sleep with her that's good, but it only means that the anger will slowly seep up to the surface. For you, who will have to wrestle with many things within you that you can't discuss with anyone, it will probably be a tall order. So the most likely outcome is that after a short while it will all go to hell.

'Okay, this is nothing to do with me. Of course I'm the craziest of all of us five, we can all agree on that. But I'm not so mentally challenged that I'm happy to see it come down on innocent kids. If you don't know what you're doing there's a high probability that Bjartur will get a traumatic shock when he sees communication between his parents break down for a second time. I can well imagine that happening, and as I say,

I don't want my activities to hurt small hearts indirectly if I can help it in any way. I myself have a grandchild of his age, as you know, and I want to be able to observe it with a clear conscience. So if I may give you a piece of advice then please, if you go to New York, have a plan.'

Solomon put his hand on Starkaður's chest and patted him, making the ash that had fallen from his cigar spread over his jacket. As The Doctor emphasized his message, Starkaður felt spittle fly in his face.

'In the first place, most importantly: you must see to it that Bjartur doesn't know you are coming, and that he will sleep over at some friends for a few days while you and Hildur are trying this out.

'In the second place, you'll turn up with a nice gift, and promise another for later in the evening.

'In the third place, be sure of one thing: underneath, Hildur is furiously angry. No matter how nice she seems, attractive, ready for sex, and so on. It's of no consequence. Of course she's angry. What you'll do is be extremely nice to her, recall things from the past, exclaim about love, and end up falling to your knees, taking off your wedding ring and offering her a new one. Together with a new beginning.

'If I'm not mistaken, this will push her far enough for her deepest emotions to come to light. In all probability she will attack you. You will hear about what you've done to Bjartur by vanishing without warning, by never coming to visit, by seldom ever getting in touch. If you get her going you should act ashamed, but still at heart remember: deep down this is a victory. At this juncture it's best that she lets off steam. You have entered the minefield, so you should tread cautiously. Show remorse, but not so much that you lose all respect. Don't say anything that has great meaning, because she will turn it all upside down and it could end with you being thrown out on the street before you know it. Let her aggression flow, agree with everything she says, show remorse. After the angry lecture, she will probably set conditions. If they consist in you having to do this or that or to make your relationship succeed, let alone having to put up with no sex until you've proven yourself, she is so angry that she is out for revenge, and this will not work. Then you can immediately make other plans. If, however, she makes it a condition that you both have to be better at communicating, you must confide your thoughts to her as they come, and then she will soon want to reconnect with her husband. But in a new and better way. Then there is hope for you, if you can hold your own.

'Let a little time pass while she calms down a bit, and then slowly begin to show a romantic interest in her. If, for example, she wants you to sleep on the sofa the first night, you will raise no objection. Praise her for her looks, flirt with her. When the lights are turned out you will lie for a while and let her be alone in bed. If you were old Almar, you would fall asleep there and the relationship might possibly recover, but never be as good as it was. Therefore, if you get this far, go into her room and put every effort into getting into bed beside her. Go easy on the emotion at this stage because she is so sensitive that romanticism could end in buckets of tears or silent desperation. Use humour, and point to an amorous past. You must quite simply seduce her at this stage. If this method works, after this prelude I would say that the relationship had a fair chance of working out. Assuming that you behave like a man. Especially if you take care to make the next few days a time of courtship and you show her great concern. If you then managed to reach out to Bjartur, that would seal it. I hope you succeed, for your sake. And even more for mine. If you get close to Bjartur and it goes well, then our work has produced something good. Are you with me, Starkaður? Do you understand where I'm going?'

'With you? Yes, I think so.'

'Good. But you should consider well what I am saying to you. You will never achieve this unless you go through it in your mind many times and prepare yourself for all the things that can go amiss.'

'May I ask you a question, Solomon?'

'Yes. Go ahead, my friend.'

'What do I do after that?'

'What do you do?'

Together they turned towards the city and looked out across the sea of light. As if the answer could be found somewhere out there. After a long pause, The Doctor said:

'I have no idea, Starkaður. In case you haven't noticed, I am not the Lord Almighty. Though I've sometimes assumed powers that are questionable, in order to make the friendly takeover succeed. But then, Starkaður, your life as Almar Logi will take over completely, and you will find out for yourself what comes next. You and your little family. I would say that you have a fifty-fifty chance of it working out. If it doesn't, then there is only one thing I will finally say. The boy must know nothing of this, and you will do better at establishing a father-son relationship with him than Almar did. Then the bond between you will be the most real thing you have in your new life, and the best justification for what we have been through with our work over the past year. The money you have lavished on us at the Firm will be pennies in your mind if you gain his love permanently. I will also say this: you can be perfectly sure that the love between you and Bjartur will be like a barometer of whether you are respecting and cultivating the reputation you bought, or whether you are abusing it.'

The Doctor turned to Starkaður again, and took him firmly by the shoulder:

'Do you understand?'

Starkaður nodded.

'I hear you.'

For a long time they looked each other in the eye, until The Doctor said:

'Enough of that, let's go in and enjoy ourselves with the hero. After all, this is his party.'

25

That night, when the farewell party was over, Starkaður sat alone, looking over the dinner table covered with overflowing ashtrays, dirty plates and bottles that had once been in the luxury price category but now cost the same as any other glass recyclables. In among the leftovers was the gift from Solomon, at once a farewell present and a kind of housewarming present. To mark that while the one was saying goodbye, the other was moving into a new life. The gift was Herodotus' *Histories* in a deluxe edition. Although Starkaður did not understand The Doctor's inscription – *to Candaules and Gyges, who despite everything were friends, and together made the Queen happy* – he knew that this was Almar's favourite book, the book he would take with him to a desert island. In the diaries Starkaður had read that he considered the work of Herodotus the best portrait of the human mind there was. The reason was that back there in the fifth century BC, when the first scientifically accepted prose work of history was written, the author described the whole of the world then known, and in doing so laid the foundations of one humanitarian discipline after another. His thinking flowed out in myths that he half believed and half doubted, allowing the reader to behold the mind of primitive man with the eyes of modern man. In the book, Gilgamesh and Enkidu merged into a single seamless person. The Doctor thought this the only suitable gift, as the work not only touched on his and Almar's common interests, but could also have a symbolic meaning for Starkaður, for the book not only gave the best portrait of the world at a certain point in time, perhaps the best portrait of the human spirit that could be found between the covers of a book, but also in connection with the friendly takeover, it symbolised the world into which Starkaður was most appropriately stepping and taking over. The world of Almar Logi. The book would be a reminder to Starkaður that he had been given a whole world, a mysterious and valuable one.

Starkaður picked up the book and was summoning up the energy to open it when there was a sound from the bathroom. He had thought he was alone in the suite and went to investigate the matter. Almar stood reflecting himself in the mirror.

'I thought you'd gone with Rita. This being the last night, and all.'

He stood in the doorway, but did not go inside. After their physical appearances had been coordinated, he found it uncomfortable to stand beside Almar in front of a mirror. A face in the mirror is just a human face, as it is. But two perfectly similar faces in a mirror show clearly that both have a certain expression, and then the question becomes which of them has the real one. When they had looked simultaneously in a mirror in the warehouse at Grindavík or in the bathroom in the attic, it was obvious which was the more youthful and optimistic. The face that was to sustain the future was inconsequential, but the other, which saw nothing ahead of it, was the real one. Sometimes it occurred to Starkaður that while Almar Logi was there, he himself was not fully present. Now he could not see Almar's face except in the mirror. With the author's mouth, the reflection said:

'How can anything grasp the human image as completely as a mirror? And while one looks at it, one is still supposed to believe that it has no hold on one, that one can move about as freely as usual. As though there were no one who could grasp the whole of one. When you look in the mirror for a long time, you feel that something is putting its arms round you. As if you were standing on the bottom of a crystal clear lake at body temperature. In the end you feel you are being embraced by another world. That's why people never spend long looking in the mirror. They move away, escape. Although, on this occasion I've been gazing for so long that soon I will push my feet against the floor and swim away from myself...'

Starkaður did not care for this speech. He strolled into the room, picked up the bottle of Camus, and sat down at the bar. Soon Almar slid in beside him. They smoked and drank in time with each other. The only difference was that Almar alone did the talking. He put his hand on Starkaður's shoulders, so that Starkaður had to make an effort not to stiffen up. With a near double in the room he became aware of something strange, of what he did not quite know. Sometimes it occurred to him that he was unusually aware of the fact that he was not unique. He reacted by being extremely preoccupied by Almar's physical appearance. If Almar wore a white shirt he did not wear a black one, because that would be too obvious a reaction, but a yellow one. If Almar had his legs crossed, he sat with his legs astraddle. If Almar was laughing, he looked reflective. If Almar was gloomy, he looked on the bright side. He often concluded that he could not escape from this annoying and obsessive comparison of them both, and at such moments felt anticipation for what might lie in the future. For the author to find the exit. After that, he had pangs of conscience and began to view Almar in terms of possible improvement. He observed certain aspects of Almar's behaviour and thought to himself that this he could do better, this he would improve... he was startled when the hand on his shoulders pulled him towards the author, who asked:

'Are you feeling remorseful?'

'Remorseful?'

'You've been a bit quiet this evening.'

'I don't know. Perhaps.'

'You don't need to be. You're just having doubts, that's all. Like about what a reputation is. What leads to a good reputation, old chap?'

'Mm, what?'

'What but a particular chain of causality, and then a little luck! The same chain of causes, without luck, may lead to a good reputation suddenly perishing. May even without warning turn into its opposite. Luck makes all the difference to people like us, Starkaður. And what is luck? It's a breath borne up from the casket of fate, a breath that may be given names like blessing, good fortune, resourcefulness, forethought or the breeze from the ever-turning wheel of fortune. Whatever luck is, then you are not ready to let the inscrutable casket's contents put an end to your story. You want to hook yourself up with a chain of causality that will produce a new word from the casket of fate.'

Starkaður studied Almar as he sat immersed in thought, talking untiringly in the spirit of the conversations with The Doctor through the night. What had become of the silent fellow who lived in the attic in downtown Reykjavik? The fellow out of whom he had to drag the words by force. Now it seemed to make no difference that he tried to indicate that he was bored by this talk – it just went on and on. As Almar continued, he even detected a trace of affection in the man's eyes:

'There is absolutely no need to feel guilty. You just think differently from most people, and that's why you're here.

You don't believe that everyone has their own story, their own unalterable deterministic past. You don't believe that time is a page on which everyone's story is written. You believe that personality can rise above its own story and since it is free it can change its history and past. Isn't that so?'

'Hmm? Well, I guess it is.'

'Exactly! And you realize that if what we're doing with the takeover is possible, there is no truth to be found in the past. Then what we want to be here and now is all there is. Excessive belief in the present moment and the ego is everywhere today. You just need to have the courage to go all the way, Starkaður, and adjust your past from the cockpit of the ego-moment. You have the courage to actualize modern man's desire to be free from history, from his own unbridled errors. I am not in a position to impede the warmest wish of the modern age for absolute freedom from the past. And I have nothing against the strong and the resourceful being able to develop at the expense of those who have contributed nothing except blinkered naivety, and never having taken any risks in a system that honours those who merely fill out a prepared schedule of how to live their lives.

Starkaður felt sure that he would never become one of those who could prattle endlessly until it sounded both like profound philosophical reflection and total gibberish. The longer he listened to the sermon, the more he hated Almar. But when he felt this, he also wanted to embrace him. Tell him to shut up and stop this childish nonsense. Suggest that they pack their bags right away and set off. They could start a new life, somewhere at the other end of the earth. He would take care of the money. Perhaps they could meet some Japanese twin sisters on Hokkaido and be neighbours who regularly dined together. If they had each other they would not even need a home country. They could even take turns to visit Iceland as Almar Logi. Their half-Japanese children would walk hand in hand to school.

But he knew he would not do this. However, he wondered why, as he wanted to. He stood up and looked long at Almar, who was in the middle of a speech which to him was a matter of complete indifference.

'What do you say we go to Japan, Almar? Now, after the earthquake and the floods, there are lots of opportunities there.'

There was no reaction. Almar continued his sermon as if to a full house of interested guests. Starkaður said good night and went to bed. He was unable to sleep, and was not surprised when Almar brought his duvet and got into the double bed beside him. For a while they lay side by side, staring out into space. Starkaður tried to bring the conversation down to earth, since he could not get rid of his double.

'I was surprised what an extrovert she is.'

'Who? Hildur?'

'When she'd had a glass or two she would always put on some old songs and drag me to my feet to dance.'

'That must have been early in the morning – Rita and I had gone by then.'

'She laughed a lot at the peacock dance, asked where the hell I'd got it from. She was very pleased to dance with me. Thought it was very "hot", and I'm quoting her literally. She said she had written me off, first as a dancer, then as a husband. That it would take a rebirth for me to get back to her. She wondered if my dancing was more like a Phoenix dance than a peacock dance. Thought it was very funny. According to her, the two of you talked much more about having another child than you told me. She said she hadn't used contraceptives

208

during the last months of your stay in New York.

'She hasn't used them since.'

'So she said.'

'So perhaps something is happening now.'

'I doubt it, she'd just had her period.'

I hope so, anyway, for your sake. Or rather, for all our sakes. Ack. I shan't sleep tonight, Starkaður. Still, it would be nice to be able to have one dream before, you know. You don't know how much I miss dreaming. The dreams I miss most are flying ones. Ones where I left my body and flew around the world. After I finally leave my body you must record my dreams. If you have trouble remembering them, you may find it useful to visit an art exhibition and then go home and rest. Just before you fall asleep you must review every picture in the exhibition until you experience it as a dream, and drift off. That way you'll get your brain in gear to remember pictures even though it's tired. When you wake up you'll remember the dreams clearly. I can't do that anymore. But you'll be able to because you believe, and dream as a result. Keep a voice recorder on your bedside table and reach out for it without moving your head, switch it on and the dreams will flow.'

Starkaður's attention wandered, and he began to think about the twin brothers' idea of freedom. Whether they were perhaps related in some way. They had come out onto the balcony to smoke when he finally replied:

'When I contemplated the prospect of imprisonment, I began to travel. I'd been travelling for several months when I realised that I was living a fantasy I'd had as a teenager. The fantasy was absolute freedom: being able to go off somewhere without a plan, without luggage, rent a car and drive away and turn wherever I want at every intersection. Stop at places that appeal to me, find accommodation, wake up in the morning and ask the waiter over breakfast what country I'm in. If there's any path down to the lake that he'd recommend. Or would I rather rent a helicopter? Or diving gear? Or order a tuxedo and a box at the opera? Always on vacation, always able to choose according to my wishes at any particular time. The whole world a plaything. Like a boy's little ball in the playground. A ball he plays with until he becomes a genius with it. I was going to have absolute freedom. I wonder if that's what you did in your dreams. Every night you left your body and flew. I have read through the dreams many times, and remarkably many of them remind me of my wanderings. The beauty we have both seen seemed to me just as aimless and uninteresting. Only the deviations were interesting. Like when you crashed in the dreams. And when I lost my grip and ended up having massage for two months, until I got to know the masseur and his family. His ridiculous life. Now if I think about the world, I see before me the everyday life of a masseur in New Delhi. Farrud got to be so relaxed with me that he let his cigarette burn beside him in the ashtray on the bench as he chatted about his mistress. Made constant fun of me and woke me every now and then to point out to me that I was having a dream I had better finish up in my hotel room. Once he came to visit me up in the suite together with his unmarried sister whom he had praised a great deal. She turned out to be the first fat Indian woman I had met.'

Starkaður smiled at the thought.

'You're right, Starkaður, all of this could easily have been in my dream. Perhaps freedom has betrayed us both. Refused to accept us and constantly kneaded us in the sick, merciless, absurd hands of life.'

They laughed and went inside to fill their glasses. As they walked into the bar they moved perfectly in time, and then raised their glasses in the same identical way, but now Starkaður found the synchronization suddenly pleasant. He put his hand firmly round Almar's neck and placed his own forehead against his. Then they stared drunkenly into each other's eyes and smiled in exactly the same way. The Doctor's parting gift lay on the bar counter. Starkaður picked it up and studied it:

'When Dr. Epstein called this a housewarming gift, I thought of an old man I met at the Imperial Hotel in New Delhi and sometimes drank with. He was a slightly peculiar long-term guest. You see, he was the hotel's former owner, and he used its historical fame after Gandhi and Nehru held a meeting there, raising the standards of the place to world-class status. When he sold it he meant to enjoy life travelling around the globe. But it worked out differently from what he expected. When the handover approached, he began to have serious concerns that the new owners would not look after long-term hotel guests adequately and didn't know how to handle the regulars, so he rented a room at the hotel for a month after he handed it over. Merely to lend them a helping hand when needed. After that he had extended his stay every month for years. I don't know why I thought of him, it was something I had on my mind...'

Towards the end of this speech Starkaður's voice slowed and fell to a whisper, but Almar seemed to understand immediately what he meant:

'Where Bjartur is concerned I'm going to be like the old hotel owner. Always renewing the booking on the suite, to remind you how to bring him up.'

'Don't worry, you've already got a long-term booking.'

'Good.'

'I even had the suite refurnished with pictures of him

211

and notebooks on what to focus on with him. That he needs help to get down from the fantasy world, back to earth and all that.'

'Good.'

When Solomon came to visit them in the morning, they were still talking. Then Almar had been talking about Bjartur for an hour, uninterrupted. As he held Starkaður's hands, he repeated how glad the boy would be when his father moved back home to New York. They were working together to return his father to him.

26

The following evening, after the farewell dinner, Clark and
Dr. Epstein said goodbye to Starkaður in the hotel lobby. The
Doctor took his farewell by giving Starkaður a long embrace
that the latter was not sure whether he found disgusting or
wished would never end. Starkaður realised that he would
never see them again. When The Doctor let him go and he
stood alone on the ice-cold marble floor, he felt an unexpected
sense of dread. He staggered, and found it odd that he was able
to keep his balance. He studied this strange father and son,
the only people who knew what he really looked like, how he
really dressed, who he really was. He addressed his words to
The Doctor:

'You know how I'll be able to find you, Solomon? I'll
just look for the owner of an orange Bugatti in the United
States.'

While Solomon laughed, Clark patted Starkaður firmly
on the shoulder and said:

'Thanks for making sure the old fellow finally gets a
new car!'

This was the first time Starkaður had seen him smile
with his eyes. He watched them get into the hired car and
drive off. Then he went up to the suite, threw himself in an
armchair in the bedroom with a new bottle of Camus, and sat
there smoking for three hours. In a bag on the bed in front of
him lay the clothes Almar had worn at the dinner party, just
like the ones he was wearing himself. He picked them up and
laid them on the bed as the author had lain in them the night
before, when they chatted about Hildur. He put Herodotus's

Histories on top of them and adjusted the sleeve to make it look as if they were holding the holy scriptures. He had drunk half the bottle when there was a knock at the door.

Framed by the ornate lintel, a depressed and tearful Rita was a sorry sight. Yet Starkaður thought she had never been more charming. Perhaps because he thought she looked more like herself than she had done at first when she knocked on his door in Thingholt, pretending to be a couch surfer. Since then he had seen her in a variety of roles. He had seen her as a flight attendant, as a horsewoman, as The Doctor's disciplined assistant who arranged tests for him, as a sexy stage director in seduction emerging from a linen drawer, as a bright-eyed and bushy-tailed guest at the saddest hotel suite party he had ever attended. Were any of these roles genuine?

She was staring into a deep void ahead of her, obviously not playing any roles at the moment. He turned his back on her, did not invite her in.

'I thought you'd gone.'

She followed him inside, and the door closed behind her.

'Without saying goodbye?'

'Yes, I thought it likely. That you were the type that preferred to simply disappear.'

She threw her red coat on to the sofa:

'Oh, don't whine, it doesn't suit you. Also, this is the last evening.'

Starkaður felt like turning round quickly and throwing his glass at her. Instead, he took a large gulp. The impact of the alcohol stirred the anger, and he wondered why he was annoyed with her. He could find no rational reason. But when he saw her at the bar counter in the hotel room, her hair dripping wet, in a red blouse, black skirt and striped tights, examining rain-sodden cigarettes, she got on his nerves unbearably. The rips in her tights, which indicated that she had walked through bushes, got on them even more. The feeling was the same as in a long-cooled love affair. He went up to her and offered her his pack of Camels.

'Sorry, I just feel rather ridiculous.'

She fished a cigarette out of the pack:

'No problem.'

Starkaður lit it for her and opened his mouth without knowing what he was going to say:

'I mean, I can't even look in the mirror to get in touch with myself. I have to see pictures of myself online to find something, something within me, and yet I feel I am looking at a dying man...'

'This is just drunk talk, stop this nonsense, Almar.'

'Almar?'

'Dear Almar.'

She smiled sadly, and stroked his unshaven cheek.

'How can you say that. Have you forgotten that night when I caught you both in the act?'

'In what act? When?'

'In the attic! When I stormed in out of the parlour after I wet my trousers with Hildur. He had his hands on your thighs, and you had your damned skirt up to the navel.'

'My dear man, you are such a fucking loser, and a big prize idiot. What do you think my job was there while Hildur was giving head?'

'To get yourself fucked, more or less.'

'You can use that word if you want. Since you can afford to. I would rather call it providing support while Almar was giving away the most precious thing he had. How do you think he felt? You're such a big fucking egotist, you wimp!'

She had been about to clear the whole bar counter, but managed only to grab a bottle of whisky that flew across onto a chair where it landed softly. Starkaður staggered over to the chair, picked up the bottle and sat down.

'But you were lovers all the time, damn it.'

She leaned wearily over her glass and blew smoke from her nostrils. She seemed to be on the point of tears, but all that came out was a silent frown. As if she were about to throw up but couldn't.

'Bloody idiot! Couldn't you at least have been fucking each other! You damn loser!'

He looked around for something to kick over. Rita was totally unmoved by his behaviour. When he realised that, all his bravado faded. She pointed at him with the glowing cigarette between her fingers:

'My job that night was to keep you relaxed. If a little massage could help to make you feel a bit better so that your eyes weren't constantly on the screen, watching your wife with another man, I felt it was okay.'

Starkaður stared at her in perplexity, and she gazed back. Her eyes were so runny that the mascara drew wavy lines down her cheeks.

He handed her a tissue and watched her remove the waves from her eyelids. She put the tissue on the table, and he picked it up and smoothed it out. It looked as though someone had written a poem on it in some ancient language. He put his glass on top of it and they began to discuss the past year. She never mentioned Starkaður by name, either referring to the 'reputation buyer' or using the name 'Almar' for them both. At first he thought it natural, as it was in concord with the agreement. However, as the evening wore on, it increasingly got on his nerves.

'Can you please call me Starkaður?'

'Not when your name is Almar.'

'Why do you always talk about us as if we were the same person?'

'Because now there is just you, Almar.'

'But Almar is dead, you saw it yourself. I mean, you held his hand and stroked his hair when he got the injection straight into a vein. Just like any other inoculation against life.'

'No, Almar, it's Starkaður who is dead. Now there is just you, Almar. We saved your life.'

He had the impression that she was falling off her chair. Was not sure if it was because she had had too much to drink or because she was having a nervous breakdown. He grabbed her and held her up. For a while she lay with her head in his lap. He thought of Almar at Súfistinn, playing chess with his son. Smiled when the boy said 'checkmate', and Almar watched him with cunning pride in his eyes. Found as he did so that his face was wet with tears. Eventually she gazed up at him. For a long time they looked each other in the eye, until she murmured:

'Kiss me, Almar.'

He had not reckoned on this command, but when he involuntarily obeyed he found that the kiss had long hung in the air without him realizing it. This was why she had not gone, like Clark and The Doctor. During the night, she kept demanding that he treat her harshly.

*

When he woke up in the late afternoon the following day she was gone from the bed. He called down to the lobby and inquired after her. She had checked out. No messages. As he held the receiver to his ear it occurred to him that everything she had told him about her past was a lie. He knew nothing about her. She, on the other hand, was the only woman who knew everything about him, and the only one who ever would. He muttered:

'I've finally met someone who is better at pseudo-identities than I am.'

He was startled when he heard the voice in the receiver say:

'Pseudo-identities? Is there anything else I can do for you, sir?'

Starkaður excused himself to the lobby assistant, said he was just reading, and hung up.

He wiped his cheek with his fingers and dried them on the pillowcase. Shook his head and sighed. Was unsure whether it was Rita he missed, Almar, or himself.

27

Having returned from Amsterdam, he staggered drunkenly up the stairs to the newly renovated attic, threw down his luggage in the parlour and lurched into the bedroom. There he lay for three days like a dead man, accumulating a pile of wine bottles, pizza boxes and noodle soup containers on top of him. The only conscious thing he did was not to answer the phone and check his email. Knew there was a danger of messing up if he had contact with people while drunk and upset. On Friday, he went out to the video rental and got a James Bond film over which he fell asleep. On Saturday, he woke up early, answered his email, sat down at the kitchen window and looked out at life in the city centre.

The week passed in reading, the watching of movies, and reflection. On the next weekend, he went to the Beer Hall, Almar's bar. He didn't have to bribe the doormen as he had at B5. The doormen knew him and called him forward out of the queue. At the bar, he managed tolerably well to cope with a large number of the author's acquaintances, especially when he used the reflective silence Almar was famous for. When they asked why they hadn't seen him for so long, he said he had written himself out of the world. Dr. Epstein had warned against consuming alcohol in public, so he drank non-alcoholic beer all evening. During the night the talk turned to the financial crash, and people began to discuss Starkaður Levi. There had been much in the news about how he was sentenced *in absentia* to seven years in jail and was now wanted by Interpol. Starkaður managed to stay out of the discussions until a husky drunk opera singer began to lash out at him for having robbed the nation. Smiling, Starkaður looked the singer in the eye and nodded, as if he knew exactly what his game was. Then leaned forward over the counter so that everyone could hear him:

'Yes, that Starkaður Levi is a jerk, you're right there, Jóhann. I also remember the days when it was all hunky dory. I happened to be at an event at the President's residence at Bessastaðir. It may have been a reception for some foreign film director in connection with a film festival or some other snobby bullshit. Anyway, I could see what was going on. There was an impoverished opera singer, who began to whisper something to Starkaður's assistant. His voice was so loud that the whisper was like a voice at ordinary volume. The assistant, who was dressed in a light blue suit that was far too big for him, kept turning away, making it look as though they were engaged in a comical dance. When the assistant trod on the hems of his trousers for the third time and was about to stumble, he gave up and asked the singer to wait. Then he sneaked away between the long dresses and the tailcoats, over to the big fish. They were clustering around the President. While the President watched cheerfully, the assistant said something to the jerk, who is now a wanted man, and then turned back to the singer. As a direct sequel to this, people around the singer drank a toast with great clamour. He had managed to cadge a two million-króna grant for himself. He knew that people did not turn down a request like that in front of the Master of Bessastaðir. The big fish had even enjoyed the opportunity of jumping and making circles in the air before the President's admiring gaze, while at the same time demonstrating their open-handedness towards the arts. The only embarrassment was that Starkaður appeared to have made it a condition that the singer should sing Steinn Steinarr's *Pauper's Song* right there and then. Which of course he did in his loud but completely soulless voice. *A real true pauper I am, a pauper who nothing can* resounded over the laughing notables. Of this recital, it must be said that the output was in perfect harmony with the input.'

Most of those sitting around the bar laughed. Starkaður watched the singer, who was gaping at him with a beetroot-red face. He smiled at the singer, and lifted his beer-glass:

'Raise a glass to the fact that those days have passed and that none of us got ensnared in that booze-up. Now we can go on the binge. Cheers!'

The Bessastaðir story brought him closer to the group, and soon he was enjoying himself, especially with the singer, who took him aside to talk about personal matters. The stories were all in one way or another about how difficult it was to be an artist. Yes, of course he had sung at prestigious opera houses around Europe. But this was still no sort of life. He spent most of his time in boring hotels between performances, and missed his children. Actually, he had received some grants in the bubble period when everything was crazy and awash with cash. Who had not? But they had mostly gone on accumulating school fees and child support debts. Starkaður noticed that he had been hypnotised by the topic of discussion when the singer said for the third time that being an artist was no sort of life, because he wholeheartedly agreed. He had begun to consider getting a shot of tequila when he thought he saw a woman he recognized appear in the crowd at the circular bar on the other side of the room. Could this be Ása? His old girlfriend? Oblivious to everything, he watched her, until the singer asked:

'Seen something that caught your fancy, Almar?'

'No, or yes, rather. That little dark one there. I remember her at Amokka on Borgartún. I sometimes used to go that way in the afternoon to find a coffee joint outside the city centre where I could write in peace. She always made me a double espresso as soon as she saw me through the window. Sometimes it was ready on my table when I went in.'

'Are you talking about Ása Tynes, who was going around with that bastard they're all talking about. Poor girl. I know her, she's nice. Come on buddy, I'll introduce you.'

Starkaður went to the bar and ordered a cosmo. Recalled that it was her favourite. When the singer had introduced them, and engaged her female friend in conversation, he said:

'You probably don't remember me at your table in the café.'

'No, actually, I don't. Not in this context. But I'm sure I would recognize you at work at once.'

'That's the fate of artists. No one ever remembers them. But I always got good service at your table. So I felt I owed you a cosmo. Here you go.'

She took the glass and leaned against the bar with the straw in her mouth. Looked at him over with a neutral expression. Her eyelashes were beautifully upward-curved, and he remembered the eyelash curler she had left in the bathroom when she moved out. She had always stood up straight and taken an untroubled view of the world, but was now slightly stooped, with wrinkles around her eyes that he didn't remember. Although she was wearing high heels she only came up to his shoulders. He wanted to stroke her lower back as he had often done when he thought she looked tired. He could not think of what to say, stuck his hands in his pockets. Opened his mouth as if to say something, and she looked at him with interest. He had almost asked if her husband had taken a job in Denmark and perhaps settled there, when he realized that would have been Starkaður speaking. He decided to keep his mouth shut. The silence became embarrassingly long. She looked likely neither to go nor to initiate the conversation. At last he half-whispered:

'Er, I think ...'

'What?'

He cleared his throat:

'Well, we all change. I mean, that's why you don't remember anything of me. But on the other hand, it suits you to be so, so...'

'Be so what?'

She was clearly amused by his hesitation. He decided to take no chances and follow the advice of The Doctor, who stressed that Almar was generally considered to lack initiative with women.

'Sorry, it's just that it makes me a little shy because I think you're so, so. What's the right word: feminine.'

'Thank you. That's exactly what I'm known for. Being a woman. And I've been one all my life, what's more.'

He remembered how mischievous she could often be, and felt cheered by it, though he restrained a smile. She took a sip through the straw, and said:

'But even though you're not very good at compliments, especially as you're an author, you were a real knight in armour to bring me a drink. Do you know that this is my favourite cocktail?'

Her expression was encouraging.

'Well, I never. Then I have a little insight into women after all.'

When they got over the embarrassment stage they found it as easy to chat as when they had been together, and soon he felt a sense of well-being he had not experienced for a long time. Ása had a presence that made him feel it did not matter if she didn't know who he really was. After they began to talk together time had flown, and before they knew it the lights were going out and people were being ushered to the exit. He thought quickly and began to talk about the new expansion of his apartment. When she showed interest, he asked her if she would like to come and have a glass of white wine at his place.

'I'm afraid I can't offer you Chardonnay.'

'Well, that's too bad, as it's my favourite white wine.'

'Right, I never guessed. I'll just have to get it for next time. But there are a lot of desirable things in the fridge. Riesling, for example. And I'd like you to teach me how to use the new coffee machine. I can't get anything out of it that matches your double espresso even halfway.'

'That's no good, we'll have to do something about it. For a start, we shouldn't talk about a machine, but a spring.'

'The coffee spring?'

'Exactly. Or best of all – the coffee fountain.'

Starkaður decided to end the evening's abstinence at home, and get drunk with her. On the sofa they were chatting enjoyably about everything and nothing when he remembered what they had been doing when they first kissed.

'Can you read palms?'

He immediately regretted the question. She took his hand and examined it.

'This is remarkable.'

Starkaður was about to pull back his hand but then she gripped it tightly with both hands. She seemed to have forgotten herself in her own reflections. Eventually Starkaður had to remind her of his presence with a clearing of his throat.

'You're a strange man, Almar.'

'Oh?'

'This is a double lifeline, like someone I once knew had.'

Starkaður used the opportunity to tug his hand free.

'Oh, who was it?'

'Alas, it's not a very romantic subject.'

Starkaður thought she was looking at him with uncomfortably thoughtful eyes.

'Tell me.'

When she replied, she had dropped the mask and was as he remembered her. To his dismay he sensed that his eyes were runny, and he began to feel for cigarettes.

'He was really the man in my life. I never thought I'd ever become a woman who'd go to the Interpol website of wanted criminals and see the man I... I once lived with.'

Starkaður knew he ought to say what? and request some sort of clarification. She looked at him searchingly, but it was a loving search, as her pupils enlarged all the way over the green colour.

'Sounds like he got mixed up in something.'

'I generally get news of him through a mutual female friend. But now there will probably be less of that after the shock she got.'

Starkaður realized that he was looking at her with enthusiasm. He gazed at his toes, which were on the table, and tried to appear indifferent.

'Actually I go to see her regularly. She recently told me that he'd dropped in on her to get a photo of us that we took on board that yacht of his. Perhaps he's somewhere in Iceland after all.'

He wanted to put his arms around her. Continue to talk about something that mattered to him. Ask her what she meant when she said his grandmother had got a shock. Instead, he picked up Almar's album of childhood photos and quickly thumbed through it. Ása seemed to notice his discomfiture, as she said:

'I'm not really the one who's looking for him all over the globe.'

'Oh, don't you miss him, then?

She seemed not to have heard the question. Looked at his lips.

'You smoke the same way he did. And actually, yes, even your lips are like his.'

She leaned closer to him and looked at his mouth. Starkaður wanted to respect her wish, and kiss her. At the same time, he was uneasy. He remembered how sensitive she was with people. He remembered that they had once been at a crowded dinner party where there was a German investor he knew rather well. After the party, she said that this ridiculous investor had done nothing but lie to them all evening. She admitted that she had only understood half of what he said, but was sure that the other half was also a pack of lies. Starkaður had not listened to her, and later it cost him tens of millions. When he asked her how she had realized this, she said she had seen it in his body language. For example, when people were remembering things, they often looked up to the left, but when they were telling fibs they usually looked up to the right. This had been the case with the investor, and she had spotted the falsehood in his words.

'Remembered something, Almar?'

He had stiffened up on the sofa beside her.

'Yes, yes indeed.'

'Well, what?'

He jumped to his feet.

'Sorry, I'm a bit under the weather. Here, have some more red wine.'

A tear crawled down his left cheek.

'Do you mind if I take a shower to freshen myself up?

I suddenly didn't feel all that great. You can look at the CD collection while I'm gone.'

In the shower, for the first time since he was a boy, he wept with racking sobs. With his bathrobe now on, he set his phone to ring after twenty minutes, and went back to the room. Ása had clearly helped herself to the red wine, as the bottle was empty. She had started to smoke, something she only did when she was very preoccupied. Her expression was the same as it had been the night she left him. Starkaður chatted light-heartedly about his pals at the bar, until the phone rang. He turned down the music, excused himself, and took the call:

'Hello, my dear, you're calling very late. What, no, no, I met Jóhann Goði at the bar. He's in *La Traviata* in Berlin just now, asked me to give you his best regards. He's in the father's role, so I thought of the two of you. What's Bjartur doing? Did he get to sleep right away? What's the time where you are ... Yes, no, I'm just about to go to bed. Then tomorrow I'm going to start packing. Is there anything you want me to buy in the duty-free store?...'

While Ása chain-smoked, he managed to simulate a five-minute telephone conversation.

After greeting her, he apologised and said he needed to go to bed, would have to wake up early. In the hallway Ása wanted to give him a goodnight kiss.

'It's a long time since I have wanted to kiss someone so much. I don't know why that is. Perhaps your unique insight into my taste in wine.'

'I want to kiss you, too, Ása. But you know how it is. I don't like to feel embarrassed when I meet the family.'

When he had closed the door behind her, he sat by the parlour window, waiting for her to come out on the pavement below. After lighting a cigarette, she looked up, blowing out smoke that spread over her like an umbrella. He stood aside, catching the curtain to stop the movement. When he glanced back, she was walking up the street in such dejection that he wanted to embrace her. He thought to himself that if his life were a dramatic love story he would run out after her in his bathrobe. When she turned towards him, fall to his knees and say he loved her. Whatever it cost, he loved her.

Then he realised that she would probably be scared out of her wits, as it would hardly be normal behaviour for a man with whom she had only spent a single evening.

He waited until she disappeared round the corner, then lit a cigarette and breathed the smoke deep into his lungs. Took out the photo of Ása on board the yacht, looked at it for a while and then burned it in the kitchen sink. When he had finished the cigarette, he turned on his laptop, connected to the Internet and booked a flight to New York for the following week.

28

Bjartur was very obedient to him right from the first day. But there was one thing he did twice every twenty-four hours. He was ready to go to bed at eight, but he always set his phone to ring at twelve and the alarm clock he had taken from the master bedroom four hours later. Invariably, just after midnight, he went into the study to check that his father was really there, and at four he entered the master bedroom and got into the bed with him. He wasn't going to let his father get away a second time. The couple had spoken to a child psychologist, who said it would be best to let the boy do as he wanted until he was sure that his father was there to stay. Hildur said he had better always be in the study at midnight and in bed by four. That was the sweetest punishment he could imagine. When he looked the boy in the face and saw how great the likeness between them was, he felt an immeasurable love for him. Nothing could match reading to the boy in his arms until he fell asleep, as usually happened when he came in at midnight. Starkaður looked at the clock above the study door. There was still half an hour until the boy arrived.

He contemplated the piles on the desk and tried to decide which project would be best to work on. There was *False Father*, the story about the bank deposit owner who pretended to be Norwegian and had a secret family in Glasgow. Next to the pile of photocopied letters lay the poetry manuscript *Passwords*, for which he had not yet been able to find a new title. Then there was *Friendly Takeover*, a collection of his own memoirs and extracts from the diaries of the reputation seller, a manuscript that gave an honest description of the process.

He sometimes thought of publishing the story of the takeover as a novel under cover of the fact that no one would ever dream that the events it described were true.

Almar's diaries for the period since his departure for New York to meet Rita and read from *Bernhard Zero* until the takeover process was completed in Amsterdam a year later lay in the middle of the table. The pile of Moleskine diaries was black, and resembled the coffin of a small, harmless creature. One evening Starkaður had promised Hildur that he was going to burn them and start a new diary, now that he had come to stay.

'Will burning the diaries change anything? she asked, surprised at his solemn tone of voice.

'It will definitely change the past for me,' he said, put his arms around her and kissed her.

Then nine weeks had passed, and the diaries were still on the table, worn and thumbed from repeated reading. The new diary lay unopened under some papers, and the fountain pen he had bought especially for it was untouched. He picked it up and tried it, but realized that it was out of ink. When he had refilled it he opened the diary, put the tip of the pen on the first page and pictured himself at Café Súfistinn. A waitress brought a ciabatta she had miss-served, and gave it to him. Immersed in his writing, he did not notice.

As he held the pen still on the page it occurred to him that it was appropriate for this diary to begin with a full stop, and raised his hand. As he contemplated what he had written he reflected that if ever a whole sentence came to him, which would be fiction no matter what he wrote, then at least the full stop at its end would be true. Thus, the truth would always follow him, even though it was small, and invisible to all but him.

It was approaching twelve. He could expect Bjartur to enter in his pyjamas, sit down on his lap and ask him to read the story in the diary. The story of the father who built a bridge across the river of his son's youth. At three minutes past, the boy opened the door. There was a small spot of wetness on his pyjamas – he had apparently been to the toilet. He sat silently in Starkaður's arms, rubbed his eyes and waited. Starkaður read slowly so he would notice when the boy fell asleep, but this time it did not happen. Bjartur listened to the story with interest right to the end:

… The boy had crossed over to the wooded slope where busy birds flew between blossom-laden branches. He realised that their singing was often the latest news, arriving through the air at lightning speed. To relax after the effort of the day he went down to the shallows where the murmur of the river drowned all other sounds, and looked into the water. Saw himself with a red beard and scarred face smiling back at him. Looked up and considered the bridge in the distance. Did not yet understand what he saw: in the middle of the bridge there was a big gap that made it impossible for him to go back. He had never crossed this gap, and yet here he was now on the wooded shore. Something had happened in the years out on the river with his father, something he would never understand.

Deep inside he knew that his father had a secret. He longed more than anything to discover what it was, but felt with agonising certainty in his heart that there was only one way to attain it: he must live his life to be as good a man as he possibly could. If he did, the mystery would be revealed to him at the moment of his death.

When the story was over, Bjartur reached for one of the diaries that lay still on the table.

'Is this a record of everything you did when you were away?'

'Well, yes, mostly.'

'Then there's a lot about me. Because you were always thinking of me.'

Starkaður did not want to give anything away, and was silent. Put his nose to the boy's curls and breathed in the familiar smell. Bjartur had started to try to read the book for himself. This made Starkaður uneasy, and he spoke to distract his attention.

'No, my boy, there's only the Bridge Story there, and I've typed it up for you so we can get someone to illustrate it for us. On the other hand, there's a lot about the illness that drew me away from you. That's why I'm just going to get rid of the diaries I wrote when I was away from home.'

Bjartur was still trying to make out the text:

'The Doctor said that we...'

Starkaður grabbed hold of the book to indicate that Bjartur should let him have it.

'It was The Doctor I had to talk to because of my illness. But now I'm well again and don't need to go anywhere.'

The boy did not let go of the book, but continued to attempt to decipher the handwriting.

'The Doctor said that we, Starl, Starkla, Starkaður and I...'

He tugged the book away from him and slammed it onto the pile on the table. Bjartur was clearly alarmed by the sudden reaction, but Starkaður pretended not to notice. He let the boy stand up. He felt that this was what he needed - to say goodbye to his time with the Small Firm. He handed the boy the pile of diaries.

'We don't want to be reminded of The Doctor and the boring time when we were separated, Bjartur. Take them and throw them all in the fire for me.'

As ever, the boy did as he was asked. He watched the flames devour one page after another and then looked at Starkaður thoughtfully. For a long time they gazed into each other's eyes until the boy turned to look at the photo in the window of his father and him on the beach at Eyrarbakki. He half-submerged in sand, the breakwater in the background. The photo was above the specially bound copy of Herodotus's *Histories*. Under the windowsill stood the chessboard. The boy went over to it and set up the pieces. This was his subtle way of not going straight back to bed after having made sure that his father was still at home. While he was setting them up, he said:

'But Dad.'

'Yes.'

'If I just make a promise to live my life and be as good as I possibly can.'

'Yes.'

'Can't you just tell me the secret now?'

'It doesn't work like that.'

'Oh, you don't trust me.'

'Yes, I do, dear boy. But you must have lived your life well to understand it.'

They played chess for a while in silence. Meanwhile, Starkaður watched him. When he had won, he said:

'Although you're my prince, you'll have to practise a lot at your computer before you can beat me.'

The boy hugged him for a long moment, looking into the fire as he did so. Starkaður felt his eyelids grow hot, and he surreptitiously wiped them on his sleeve. Whispered:

'I'll tell you the whole story on my deathbed. After that, you can choose whether you want to own the world or the truth about it. But then you must hold my hand all the time. Do you promise?'

'I promise.'

They looked each other in the eye.

'You mustn't let go, no matter how the story ends.'

'I promise, dear Dad.'

He hugged the boy again, now even harder. As if to hold back the tears. Then he saw the boy to bed, spread the covers over him and kissed him good night. When he had closed the bedroom door, he began to return to the study but changed course when Hildur called to him to come to bed.

We hope you've enjoyed this contemporary novel by Bjarni Bjarnason and are inspired to try out other books in our fantastic range of authors...

Having the book translated was inspired by our commitment to bring the very best of the world of less well-known writers to an English-reading world.

As well as poetry we also publish fiction, translations, travel and history at Red Hand Books so please go to our website at :

www.redhandbooks.co.uk

to find out more and support independent publishers and booksellers.

Thank you for your support.
Everyone at Red Hand Books